A BILLIONAIRE DENTIST *for* Christmas

dobi daniels

Luxhaven
Publishing

ISBN paperback, 978-1-958987-03-2

Interior Design by Luxhaven Publishing

Cover Design by The Book Brander Boutique

Editing by JD Book Services

Proofreading by Lisa Lee Proofreading

To JC, Grandma D, and DC, whom I love more than life itself.

Dexington Christmas Billionaires Series

A Billionaire Inventor for Christmas

Her Billionaire Butler for Christmas

Her Billionaire Dentist for Christmas

Dexington Doctor Billionaires Series

Loving The Billionaire Heir Doc

Loving The Billionaire Owner Doc

Loving The Billionaire Army Doc

Loving The Billionaire Boss Doc

Loving The Billionaire Cowboy Doc

A Cowboy Loves the Doctor Series

A Doctor Second Chance for the Rancher (prequel)

A Doctor Blind Date for the Cowboy

A Doctor Enemy for the Cowboy

A Doctor Billionaire for the Cowboy

Standalone

Her Billionaire Nemesis (short story)

SEE ALL OF DOBI DANIELS BOOKS

at https://dobidaniels.com.

AUTHOR'S NOTE

Thank you for choosing A BILLIONAIRE DENTIST FOR CHRISTMAS. I enjoyed writing the story of Veronica Brooks and Jude Stone, two very interesting characters!

It's so easy to believe your circumstances and past define who you are, making you unworthy of love. I pray A BILLIONAIRE DENTIST FOR CHRISTMAS gives you the hope and courage to believe in yourself no matter what and permit yourself to love again.

Would you like to be notified when the next Dobi Daniels book releases? Sign up at https://dobidaniels.com.

Once again, thank you so much for purchasing
A BILLIONAIRE DENTIST FOR CHRISTMAS
and for meeting Veronica Brooks and Jude
Stone. If you enjoyed it, please consider leaving
a review at your favorite retailer or recom-
mending it to a friend.

Thanks again for your support!

Dobi Daniels

A BILLIONAIRE DENTIST for Christmas

CHAPTER 1

TWENTY-TWO YEARS AGO

*J*ude Stone leaned against the old tree in the hospital's back garden and kicked hard at a rock at his feet. He watched it roll away and then land in a muddy puddle with no way to get out. Just like how he felt about his life right now. He was mad at the world and at the father that had abandoned him.

He'd told himself over and over again that it wasn't his fault. Being born with a cleft palate—which was what the doctors had called it—and having to go through multiple operations wasn't something he'd wanted. He'd even had a bone graft a few weeks ago and was still recovering. Jude had come to the hospital with his mom today for a follow-up. His mom had wanted to speak with the doctors alone, so Jude had ended up in the garden that was as familiar to him as his home.

Jude frowned. The Christmas lights strewn over the flower hedges like twinkling stars fallen from the sky were yet another reminder of his loss. The hospital had hosted a "Christmas time with Santa" for the kids a few days ago, and with his father as the designated Santa Claus, Jude had had no choice but to come along with him to the party. If he'd known his father would disappear on them shortly after that, maybe he would have asked for his father as his Christmas gift instead of the small car he'd received. Now, any joy he'd felt from the toy was gone. He kicked another stone. What terrible luck he had.

But his heart ached even though it'd been a few days. How could his father, who was supposed to be there for him and hold his hand, just leave? To be fair, his father wasn't the hand-holding type, but still. Instead, all his father had done was leave a note for his mom, who tried to hide her tears and only let them out when she thought Jude wasn't looking. He hated to see her cry.

He kicked hard at another rock. This time, it rolled and then stopped in front of a pair of pink shoes. Jude looked up to see a girl a little younger than him, with her hair done up in braids and colorful ribbons, staring at him with big brown eyes. She was dressed in a pink coat over a yellow dress that stopped at her knees and held a lollipop in each hand. The girl looked happy, the opposite of the way he felt right now.

Jude winced as his heart squeezed in pain. All he wanted was for her to go away. "What?" he said in his harshest voice, though he was sure it came out more nasal and jumbled up than he'd wanted. Cleft palate did that to you, even though he'd been seeing the speech doctor.

"Do you want one?" She extended one of the lollipops to him with her left arm. Jude noticed she had a mole there.

"Go away. Leave me alone," he replied.

"It will make everything better," she insisted.

It wouldn't bring his father back, that was for sure. "Go," he said.

Instead, she stepped forward and leaned her back against the same tree.

Jude stared at her in surprise. She was bold.

How could she do that when she didn't even know him?

The girl gave him a cheeky smile in return and offered him the lollipop again.

This time, he just shook his head and opened his mouth to show her the stitches.

"Oh, that's okay," she said. "You can eat it later." She stuffed the lollipop into his hand without asking.

Jude allowed his hand to close around the lollipop. It seemed she wasn't scared of his mouth. He was used to other kids laughing at him about it. But she was treating him like he was any other normal kid.

They stayed that way, he kicking the stones, she licking her other lollipop. Jude realized he didn't mind her presence as much as he had in the beginning.

"I'm an orphan," she said suddenly.

Jude gawked at her. He would never have believed it. She was dressed like someone had taken the time to get her ready. If not her parents, then who? And how did she manage to look so happy?

"Martha takes care of me," she said as if sensing his unspoken question.

Who was this Martha? A guardian? An aunt? She had to be kind since the girl didn't look sad at all.

"My father left." Jude didn't know what made him say it, but somehow he wanted her to know.

"But you have your mommy," she said in a wistful tone.

Yes, he did. But how did she know? She must have seen him with her. It was so easy to forget he still had any good despite the bad. He'd been so upset that his father left, but here was a girl who had neither parent yet seemed cheerful. Maybe he could be happy too.

"Here, take this," she said. Jude looked to see she was holding a pendant hanging from a braided necklace. The pendant looked like a bird with its wings spread out. She must have had it tucked under the neck of her dress.

He shook his head. It was hers. She didn't have to give it to him.

"Martha gave it to me for good luck. Take it," she said.

He shook his head again and turned away. He wasn't a charity case. Jude didn't need pity from anyone.

She grabbed his hand, stuffed the pendant into it, and took off, her braids bouncing behind her.

"Hey!" he called out.

She turned, waved at him, and then hurried off until she disappeared through the doors that led into the hospital.

Jude looked down at the pendant in his hand. It was now one half of the bird with the braided cord. She must have taken the other half. The grooves on its body flowed out into its remaining wing, giving it a life-like appearance, a proud posture as if it didn't matter that it had lost its other wing.

He rubbed his thumb over the surface of the bird for a while as a cool breeze caressed his face. Then he lifted the cord and slipped it over his neck. Jude had lost one wing, his father, but that didn't mean his life was over. He was going to soar and be whatever he wanted, just like the bird.

He would make his life count, father or no father.

Jude straightened from the tree, tucked his hands into his black coat, and headed back in the direction of the hospital's doorway, the faint sounds of "The First Noel" reaching out to him from between its glass doors.

He hoped he'd see the girl again, to thank her. But the hospital was a big place, and chances were he'd never meet her again.

All the same, Jude prayed he'd get the opportunity one day to return the favor.

CHAPTER 2

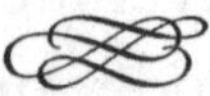

PRESENT DAY

*V*eronica Brooks slammed the door of her apartment and hurried down the steps. Early morning mist hung low in the air, and Veronica shivered as her gym shoes hit the cobblestone sidewalk. It was colder than she'd have expected in the third week of November.

She was late. How could she have overslept today of all days? She'd been looking forward to a run near the river all week and was even more desperate for it now after the call she'd just received. Dr. Fuller, her colleague and partner in the dental practice they co-owned, had called to inform her about an impromptu business meeting this morning.

Business meetings were nothing new at their

dental practice. The clinic typically held one monthly to review the non-thrilling aspects of running the business, and to plan for the upcoming month—the next one was due in seven days. So why would Dr. Fuller schedule one today? Unless he had urgent information to share that couldn't wait. His voice had sounded grave on the phone, so Veronica worried it might be unpleasant news. She'd tried to get him to open up about it, but he'd insisted he'd update her at the meeting.

She ran a hand over her hair even as she avoided some of the brown leaves that had fallen overnight from the almost bare trees that stood like sentries along the street. For goodness sake, she didn't need any bad news this close to Christmas. She'd been looking forward to taking some time off and enjoying all the Christmas activities the orphanage—where she was raised—had planned for the season. But now Veronica feared whatever Dr. Fuller planned to discuss at the meeting would change everything.

She flipped the hood of her sweatshirt over her head as she took off and settled into a quick jog around the neighborhood. Veronica loved the clinic. Dr. Fuller had started the practice thirty years ago on Dexington's Bakers Street, a busy area where local mom and pop businesses occupied every two buildings or so and a favorite gateway into the suburbs. Fuller Dental was a popular choice for surrounding neighbor-hoods and had maintained a steady influx of patients over the years.

Veronica had joined the practice right after her pediatric dentistry residency. With her skills complementing Dr. Fuller's expertise in both general dentistry and orthodontics, they'd been able to handle most of their patients' dental needs and referred the rest to applicable special-ists. Dr. Fuller had eventually offered her a stake in the practice, and Veronica now owned thirty percent of it.

But patient traffic had been declining over the past months. The clinic provided excellent services, but their office sorely needed an upgrade, and all her suggestions to Dr. Fuller on how they might improve the practice had fallen on deaf ears. Though Dr. Fuller was a kind gentleman and a great dentist, he was set in his ways and saw no reason to alter what had worked well for him over the years. But times had changed, and Veronica worried their clinic might become obsolete if they didn't make adjustments soon. Then her fears began to come true.

First, a large one-stop dental business moved in two streets over and offered dental services at rock-bottom prices. A good number of Veronica's patients had switched over to them. The new business had folded up a few months later —not surprising given their unsustainable prices—and only through the diligence of Veronica and her dental team in reaching out to their former patients had most returned. But Fuller Dental needed to make changes if it wanted to keep its patients. She'd thought the incident would be a wake-up call to Dr. Fuller, but he'd dismissed her concerns.

Now they were seeing an efflux again to a new competitor that had opened shop the next street over. This time, it seemed the business was here to stay. Though Veronica hadn't visited the place, she'd heard from some patients and the other business owners on her street how wonderful the new clinic was, their prices on par with what Fuller Dental charged. The owner of the place was said to be an oral and maxillofacial surgeon, a certain Dr. Stone.

She'd felt a jolt of envy at the news. Veronica wished she had the funds to create and run a dental clinic the way she would have liked, but establishing a dental practice was very expensive. She was grateful to Dr. Fuller for offering her a stake in the business—Veronica had been lightyears from owning one. He'd given her a chance to make payments over time, and the experience she'd gained so far in running a dental clinic was invaluable. Even so, she hoped Dr. Fuller's news didn't have anything to do with the clinic's declining business.

Veronica checked her watch and let out a sigh. Her run had been far too short, yet she needed to start heading back if she was going to make it to work on time.

She pulled out the red stress ball she kept in the pocket of her sweatshirt. Veronica's right hand had taken to aching recently and squeezing the ball on her runs tended to help. She closed her eyes for a second and exhaled. She had to believe everything would work out no matter what Dr. Fuller's news was.

Something heavy crashed into Veronica. Her eyes flew open, and her arms flailed in an effort to find support. But there was nothing to grab onto, and she landed on her backside on the cobblestone.

Ouch! Veronica hoped her tailbone was not broken. What just…?

Her eyes widened in shock as a large slobbering tongue began to lick her face. The most beautiful dog she had ever seen, with a silver-grey coat and warm blue eyes, was lapping up her face like she was the most delicious ice cream he'd ever tasted. She couldn't help the laughter that bubbled up from her throat. Veronica had always wanted a dog, but she hadn't expected to become a treat for one.

"King, get off her!" a deep masculine voice commanded.

King? For goodness sake, who named their dog King?

The dog whined but obeyed, and then the dog owner came into view.

Well, well, well. If the dog was King, what would she call the owner that looked so delectable she could just stare at him all day? The beautiful—yes, beautiful instead of handsome—man standing in front of her looked at her with concern oozing from his warm brown eyes. Tall with his hair cut longer at the top and tapered on the sides, he wore a short well-groomed beard that finished off his polished masculine look.

The real-life Adonis extended a hand to her. "I'm so sorry about the dog. Let me help you up."

Her eyes couldn't help glancing at his ring finger. No ring. But that didn't mean he wasn't married—types like him never stayed long on the single market.

Veronica accepted his hand but almost let go from the immediate electric sparks that shot through her arm at their touch.

Hello! What was that? This man was supposed to be a total stranger. She had no business feeling this way with him.

"Are you okay?" he asked, oblivious to the thoughts that were running through her mind.

Her eyes darted to his lips as he spoke, and she almost melted. Veronica had never seen such kissable lips on a guy before. Gosh, he was really beautiful. And those black gym clothes? They fit his olive frame like a glove.

Cool your jets, honey, she scolded herself. *Since when did you start swooning over guys?* But there was nothing wrong with appreciating God's own creation, another part of her reasoned. It wasn't like she planned on marrying him here and now.

Veronica had learned the hard way that luck was not on her side when it came to dating or marriage. The two men she'd dated had both dumped her during different Christmas seasons. The first fellow had met his childhood crush during a Christmas carol service and had promptly gotten engaged that same night without breaking up first with Veronica. Veronica had heard about it later from some acquaintances.

The second guy had even proposed. But when he'd introduced her to his mom during Christmas dinner, she'd treated Veronica like scum because she'd grown up an orphan, information Veronica had never hidden. He'd called it quits the same day via text. Maybe being abandoned as a baby on the steps of St. Andrews orphanage during Christmastime had jinxed her for life.

Since staying in bed and crying into her pillow was not Veronica's idea of how to spend Christmas, she'd chosen to fly solo ever since, even though she held out hope each year that her jinx might be broken. Yet she wasn't sure her heart could risk it.

But her body seemed to disagree. Veronica felt her face flush with warmth and was glad for once that it wasn't usually obvious to most people. "I'm fine," she managed to say.

She allowed him to pull her to her feet and then brushed away the dirt on her backside. Still, the front of her outfit was dirt-stained courtesy of slobbering King, who looked like a sweetheart with his big round eyes and large ears. He had Veronica's red stress ball in his mouth, and she had a feeling she'd never be able to get it back. She tested her wrists and ankles—everything seemed to be in working order.

Her digital watch beeped. Veronica glanced at the time. *Shoot!* She was running late.

She had to leave, both to protect her heart and not be late for her meeting. However, a small part of her wished she could just stay and get to know more about this man who was having such a magnetic effect on her.

She bent and patted King who had sat on his haunches. Veronica was surprised to see King make eye contact in return. "See you later, King."

She straightened and turned to the man. "I have to go," she said and took off at a brisk pace without waiting for his response.

"Wait!" the man called out.

Veronica ignored him and broke into a run instead. She needed to put as much distance as possible between them before her resolve weakened. It was time to forget the man and focus on her upcoming meeting with Dr. Fuller.

But a part of her wondered if she'd made a mistake by leaving him behind.

CHAPTER 3

*J*ude stared after the young woman that was sprinting away from him. What had just happened? He'd been shocked when King jumped her. The dog was usually wary of strangers and went out of his way to avoid them, so Jude had wondered at first if he'd met her before.

But the almond-shaped eyes with sweeping eyelashes that had stared back at him had been unfamiliar yet had managed to seize his attention. She was beautiful and striking with warm brown skin that glowed with the richness of life and had dark luscious hair with a little bit of spring in it. It was like his whole being came alert. Then he'd heard her voice. The lyrical sound had swirled right to his core and turned him inside out. When he'd reached out to help her to her feet, the sparks that he'd felt had been electrifying.

Who was she, and why was she having such an effect on him? For the first time, Jude was glad he was back in Dexington. He and his mom had left many years ago, and he'd spent most of his young life in California where he'd gone to college, dental school, and residency to become an oral and maxillofacial surgeon—and a wealthy one at that.

Jude had been lucky to have a college roommate who was fascinated with inventing devices, and together they'd opened a medical device company with their joint creations. Fortunately, they'd held off on selling the company early and had waited until the business valuation had grown. Then they'd taken it public before they were eventually acquired by a leading medical device company. Despite the grueling work to make both the company and his residency training work, it had been worth it, and Jude had netted hundreds of millions of dollars which, through strategic investments, had turned Jude into a billionaire. But the best part of the wealth he'd acquired was it allowed his mom to retire. She'd worked so hard all her life to support him and could now follow whatever dreams she had.

But being rich also brought its share of problems. Jude and his business partner had been featured in newspapers and magazines, and Jude had ended up with more than a few stalkers. So when his mom had suggested a return to Dexington, Jude had been amenable to the idea.

So far it had worked out well, and Jude felt like he had returned to his days of anonymity. The small city gave him the small-town feel he'd missed yet was close enough to big cities like New York and Boston. He'd opened the dental practice of his dreams where patients were guaranteed a wonderful experience. Given the amount of dental work he'd had in childhood, Jude had always wished he'd had it easier. So now, he tried to soften the trauma for others by providing a welcoming environment in his clinic.

His practice had weekly themes based on popular cartoon or TV show characters, and his pediatric patients were allowed to vote on them a month ahead of time. The kids could also make fun suggestions for each week via a suggestions box. Jude tried to incorporate those as much as he could. Once the theme was selected, it got reflected in the staff's outfit for the week and in the clinic decor—Jude had a team responsible for managing the transitions.

Patients were also treated to surround music, and their choice of either watching a movie or kiddie program using tablets, or getting a foot massage and pedicure while waiting. The kids also had a huge play area in a corner of the lobby. Treatment involved the best dentists, hygienists, and dental assistants he could hire, who then administered care using state-of-the-art equipment fit for royalty. And all of these did not cost extra. Yet Jude managed to maintain an efficient and effective patient workflow. So it was no surprise that even patients from other towns were drawn to his clinic.

But being back in the town had reopened old wounds, memories of his childhood he'd rather have kept buried. He'd bought a house in the wealthy part of town, a far cry from where he'd previously lived with his mom, and that seemed to have helped in avoiding his previous haunts. Even when he'd mistakenly ended up at a grocery store he and his mom used to frequent, no one had recognized him, and for that he was grateful.

But his first Christmas since he'd returned was now approaching. Jude had begun to feel unsettled. Christmas was not his favorite time of the year after his father's abandonment, and he tried to avoid the festivities as much as possible. Unfortunately, the Dexington community was well-known for them. In addition, his mom hoped to be involved this time around—she'd held off on celebrating Christmas all those years in California because of him. Sure, they'd bought Christmas presents for each other, but that was all they'd done. Since this year promised to be different, Jude wasn't sure how he would survive the season. So his mind had been preoccupied with those thoughts when King had crashed into the beautiful lady.

There was something about her that called to him, and he longed to know her more. But as she faded out of view, other thoughts assaulted his mind. What if this was all a set up? Anyone who was familiar with Jude would have known that King had a thing for red balls. What if she'd targeted him? Jude had run this route since he'd come back, and anyone tracking him would have known he'd pass this way with King.

Jude let out a sigh. He was tired of gold diggers and stalkers. Jude had been unlucky in relationships so far—they either wanted him for his money or exhibited obsessive behaviors—so he'd closed his heart to love. Even if this woman wasn't either, he had to remain cautious about who he let into his life. The last thing he needed was a repeat of what had happened in California.

His mood spoiled, Jude figured it was time he headed back home. He had a busy day ahead of him, and that was what he needed to focus on. As well as how to get through Christmas unscathed. Thinking about the beautiful lady didn't fit into his agenda for the day.

"Let's go, King," he said as he put the dog's leash on and began his run back home.

It was time to forget her.

CHAPTER 4

"I'm sorry, Dr. Brooks, but we may need to consider closing down or selling the practice by the year's end."

Veronica's heart beat loudly in her chest at Dr. Fuller's words. Sure, she'd expected sales this month to be bad, but not this horrendous. Now he was thinking of giving up.

Dr. Fuller ran a hand over his salt and pepper hair. He was usually so calm and collected—this was the first time Veronica had seen him so frazzled. Deep lines of worry furrowed his forehead. Sheila, the office manager who'd worked for Dr. Fuller from the beginning, was also seated in the small bland conference room where the meeting was taking place, and she looked sad. Sheila handled all the billing, dental insurance, and treatment co-ordination work and made sure the office ran efficiently on a day-to-day basis.

"I'm sorry, Dr. Brooks," he said in a softer tone. "This wasn't how I planned this would go. I'd thought I'd be turning the practice over to you in a few years. But I might be getting too old for this, and after the health scare two weeks ago, Mary is pushing for me to retire. As much as I'd hate to do this, I'm not sure there's any other alternative. Of course, I'll make sure your investment in the clinic is returned." Mary was Dr. Fuller's wife of over thirty years, and she was right to be concerned about his health.

But this wasn't what Veronica needed. She loved this clinic, its patients, the staff and couldn't imagine letting it go. Shutting the clinic's doors would mean losing everything she'd worked hard for over the past few years. And it would surely break Dr. Fuller's heart to let his precious clinic go like this.

Veronica didn't have enough funds to buy him out or the collateral needed to be able to get a business loan. Though her best friend, Sarah Dexington, was married to one of the richest men in the city, Veronica wasn't about to take advantage of the friendship. She had to do this on her own. She'd raised herself and worked hard throughout the years to get to where she was, and taking the easy way out was not an option.

Most of all, she believed the clinic was still viable and could be made more profitable again. "What if I can raise the clinic's revenue before year end? Would you change your mind?" Veronica asked. She had no plan yet, but she hoped to come up with one.

A small ray of hope dawned in Dr. Fuller's eyes, but then he frowned. "How would that be possible? It's only a few weeks away."

"But what if I can make it happen?"

Dr. Fuller leaned forward. "If you can, I'll reconsider it. It would give me some ammunition to convince Mary to change her mind."

"And you'd let me do what I want?" She'd need free rein to make any upgrades she deemed fit.

"Sure, as long as you don't break the bank."

Fair enough. "Thank you," she said.

The meeting ended, and Veronica left the

room. Her thoughts were all over the place, and she didn't know where to begin.

A hand touched her arm, and she turned. It was Sheila, every strand of her snow-white bob that framed her oval face in place as usual. "It's going to be alright," she said.

Veronica nodded and swallowed the lump in her throat.

"Let's grab a cup of tea," Sheila suggested and steered Veronica in the direction of the coffee room. The yellow colored space did nothing to cheer her spirits. Once they were seated and sipping the hot cinnamon-infused tea, Sheila turned her intelligent blue eyes on Veronica. "Do you have any ideas in mind?" she asked.

"I figured we'd start with the few cosmetic changes that are easy fixes," Veronica said. "Maybe new paint colors on the walls, exposing and refinishing of the hardwood floors, redecoration of the waiting room."

"I can arrange the paint job and the refinishing of the hardwood floors," Sheila said.

"I'll handle the redecorations."

"I expected you would," Sheila said with a smile. "You've always been good with that."

Which was true. Veronica was known for changing the look of her apartment every season, and she managed to accomplish it each time on a limited budget.

"But that won't be enough." Veronica took a sip of her tea before continuing. "I need to come up with a solid plan to draw new patients in."

"I have a suggestion," Sheila said.

"What is it?"

"Why don't we visit the new dental place?"

Veronica couldn't believe she'd heard right. "You mean Toothy Grin Dental?" Even now, she couldn't get over the name of the dental place that had lured away so many of their patients. But what was Sheila thinking?

"Yes. But hear me out first." Sheila took another sip of her tea. "We need to see what they're doing differently. Not only have they been successful in drawing in patients in the area, I've heard young families from all over Dexington are beginning to go there as well. They have to be doing something right."

Oh. Veronica hadn't known that. Fuller Dental had tried before to reach patients from all over Dexington, but most had stated a desire to stick with their neighborhood dental clinics.

What was it about this new clinic that was reaching that customer base? Sheila was right that they had to find out. "Okay, I'll think about it."

"How about now?"

Veronica raised an eyebrow. "Now?"

"Mm-hmm. Unless you have something pressing you need to take care of?"

Veronica exhaled. Sheila was hardly pushy. But when she was convinced about something, nothing could deter her until she achieved what she wanted. It was part of what made her great at her job. Veronica's best option was just to give up and go with it. Besides, she had nothing on her calendar until afternoon—Sheila had rescheduled all their morning appointments because of the meeting. "Okay." She finished her tea and rinsed off the cup in the sink.

"Great. I'll go with you."

"What about the office?" Veronica asked.

Sheila waved her concern away. "Tami will handle it just fine." Tami was the receptionist that answered the phone and handled all the patient appointments. "The fresh air would do me good. Besides, we'll be back soon."

Veronica returned to her office to grab her coat

and then waited outside the clinic entrance for Sheila to join her. The sun had come out, yet it wasn't hot enough to drive away the chill in the air. Veronica tucked her hands into her coat pockets. No matter how long she'd lived here, she still wasn't used to the cold. Yet she couldn't imagine living anywhere else. Dexington was home for her, and she loved the quaint and picturesque city, with its brick-lined streets and colonial structures that dated back centuries. Of course, there was the occasional modern building here and there, but they only added to the charm of the small city.

"I'm ready." Veronica hadn't even noticed when Sheila came out. She was wearing an oversized red coat over her petite frame, yet it looked cute on her.

They made their way down the building steps and onto the cobblestone sidewalk. Soon they passed large trees that lined either side of the street and shaded parked cars from the mid-morning sun as they headed toward the main avenue. The air was crisp and nippy, so Veronica turned up the collar of her coat.

"So what are your plans for Christmas?" Sheila asked.

"Same as usual," Veronica responded. "I plan to spend most of it at the orphanage. What about you?"

"The whole family is coming into town. I'm looking forward to seeing my great-grandbabies." Sheila had married early and already had grandchildren who had finished college. Veronica had attended the marriage of the first of them two years ago. Sheila hadn't been able to travel when her granddaughter had twins a few months ago.

"That must be nice."

"It is. Having family is great. You need your own too."

"I already have mine," Veronica replied. "The kids at the orphanage are my family."

"True. But you need a man of your own."

Veronica already knew that. But good men couldn't be plucked from trees. "I'm doing just fine," she said instead.

Sheila gave her a sharp glance. "Keep telling yourself that. You need a good man who'll love you wholeheartedly."

Veronica didn't blame her—Sheila was lucky and had been married for fifty-five years to her sweetheart who adored her to this day. "I'm working on it," she replied.

Sheila placed a hand on her arm, and Veronica stopped and turned to her. "You need to keep your heart open," Sheila said. "I know you've received more than your fair share of hurt, but there's a good man out there who'll appreciate just how special you are."

Veronica said nothing but turned her face away. Then she began to walk again.

Sheila only meant well, but she didn't understand that every time Veronica had been rejected, she'd felt like she'd been abandoned all over again. It was a painful experience, and she wished she could just be like everyone else and brush it off easily. So now she was afraid to try. Who would want to go through that hurt again? Veronica used to believe what Sheila had said, but these days she wasn't sure anymore.

They continued on in silence and soon reached the street where the new clinic was. Veronica stopped a few feet from its entrance. The commercial building was already decked out in intricate green, silver, and gold Christmas decorations with a snowman in complete winter attire by the door, giving the office a cheery and welcoming vibe.

Sheila's eyes widened. "Wow! This looks pretty!"

Now how did they manage to have an honest-to-goodness snowman when no snow had fallen so far this year?

"I heard a company delivers the snowman each morning," Sheila said as if she'd read Veronica's thoughts. "The clinic put up a bulletin board and asked kids to vote for their favorite Christmas decoration, and the snowman won hands-down. So now the owner makes sure there's a fresh snowman with a new outfit every day. I heard the kids love it, and I can understand why after seeing it for myself."

Only Sheila would know all these details—she had a way of remaining up-to-date on everything that happened in their neighborhood.

The place looked nice without appearing gaudy. Maybe Veronica could borrow the idea and have Christmas decorations that fit with their brand set up at Fuller Dental. It was something to think about.

"Okay, let's go inside." Sheila looped her arm with Veronica's.

Veronica let go of Sheila's arm and dug in her heels. "I don't think that's a great idea," she said. Sure, it was what they'd planned to do, but now she wasn't so certain it was the brightest move. What if she met patients that recognized her?

Something knocked into her from behind, and Veronica lost her footing and went flying in the air and landed in someone's arms. From the corner of her eye, she spied someone in a hoodie racing away from her down the sidewalk.

"Are you okay?" the voice she'd never expected to hear again asked.

Veronica froze for a second and then looked up. Those warm brown eyes she could never forget stared back at her in surprise. He was now dressed in a blue button-down shirt and grey slacks that did nothing to conceal his fit frame. Of all coincidences, she had landed in the arms of the handsome stranger! Her face and neck grew impossibly hot. What were the odds of meeting him here?

"Dr. Stone?" a voice called out.

Veronica and the man both looked in the direction of the voice. A young lady dressed in colorful scrubs had just stepped out through the double doors of Toothy Grin Dental. "Yes?" the man answered.

Dr. Stone? He was a doctor? Now why did that name sound familiar? For some reason, the crash into the stranger's arms seemed to have shorted the workings of her brain.

"Your patient is ready for you in your office," the lady said.

Hold on one second! He was a dentist? Then it came to her: Dr. Stone, oral and maxillofacial surgeon and owner of Toothy Grin Dental.

The one responsible for stealing away her patients.

Her enemy.

She'd been caught up in the hands of her enemy.

Veronica sprang from his arms as if she'd been bitten by a snake.

"Veronica, are you alright?" Sheila cried out and reached for her.

"I'm fine. We need to go." Veronica didn't wait for Sheila's response but strode back in the direction from which they'd come. But her heart thudded in her chest like she'd run a marathon. Why did it have to be him of all people? She was mad at herself for even holding onto a small hope that this Christmas might have been different if she'd given herself a chance to know him better. How could life be so cruel as to allow the man who'd stolen her business a chance to steal her heart too?

Well, that wasn't going to happen, or her name wasn't Veronica Brooks. Besides, this was the straw that broke the camel's back. She'd kept quiet long enough about losing their patients to Toothy Grin Dental, and it was time she did something about it.

"Are you okay?" Sheila asked as she caught up with her.

She'd forgotten about Sheila. "I'm sorry," Veronica said. She slowed down her pace so that Sheila could walk by her side.

"What happened back there?"

"Don't worry about it." Sheila gave her a look but said nothing else. They continued back to the office in silence.

But Veronica's thoughts couldn't stop churning. She, Veronica Brooks, was going to get back her patients and then some. Dr. Stone couldn't say he hadn't known Fuller Dental was on the next street over when he'd opened the place. He'd declared war by doing so.

So she was going to show him it was the worst mistake he'd made. She'd do it all fair and square too.

Veronica was going to come up with a great idea no matter what it took.

She would show Dr. Stone what happened when a lioness got cornered.

CHAPTER 5

*J*ude watched as the woman walked away from him a second time. How was it possible she was here merely a few hours after he'd only met her? Again, the likelihood that she might be stalking him occurred to him.

He had to admit she'd felt good in his arms, and her soft gardenia scent had almost brought him to his knees. She'd been soft in all the right places, even with the air of fragility he'd sensed about her.

Veronica—that was what the older woman by her side had called her. It was a beautiful name, fitting for such a gorgeous lady. Jude had fought the urge to draw her closer every second she'd been in his arms. But maybe he was feeling this way because it'd been a while since he had been in a relationship.

A previous girlfriend had been all nice and good until he'd overheard her confessing to her friend that she was only with him for the money. Jude had ended the relationship immediately. He'd thought his last girlfriend was the one until she'd become too obsessed with him to the point of stalking. Jude had closed off his heart since then, and no one else had caught his attention.

Until now.

But why had Veronica come to his clinic? It didn't seem like she was a patient—she'd halted on the sidewalk despite the older woman urging her to go in. That wasn't a typical reaction for Jude's patients, who were only too happy to come in for their appointments. Had she known he owned the place?

Someone had knocked into her, pushing her into his arms. Was the person her accomplice? Maybe someone had been watching and seen when Jude had gone to the car and timed her arrival such that he'd be forced to catch her in his arms.

But then why had Veronica jumped back after hearing his name? Jude had to admit he'd felt the loss immediately. Or was this the new stalking tactic: get him all confused until he lowered his defenses enough for her to worm her way into his life? He had to admit Veronica was succeeding if that was her strategy. But he would not let it go further than this, no matter how much a part of him was curious to learn more about her.

"Dr. Stone?" It was Kathy, his dental assistant, who'd stepped out to look for him. Jude had gone to his car to pick up a journal only to realize he'd left it at home.

"I'll be right there," he replied and headed toward the clinic's entrance.

Whatever her story was, it was time to forget about Veronica and take care of the patient that was waiting for him.

Jude hoped he'd never see her again.

CHAPTER 6

Veronica gazed out at the Fuller Dental staff that had gathered round the small conference room table. She'd asked the team to arrive an hour early, and they'd complied. All hands were needed on deck for her idea to work—she'd scrambled out of bed in the early hours of this morning just to make sure she'd written down every single detail. The only person missing was Dr. Fuller—he'd taken his wife to the hospital for her annual check-up. But Veronica had already spoken to him about her project, and he was on-board with it.

"I have a plan I believe would help us increase sales before Christmas and hopefully after," Veronica started. "Dr. Fuller has already given us his go-ahead, so that shouldn't be a problem."

"What is it?" Angela asked. Angela was the dental hygienist that handled most of the preventive dental care work at the clinic. The buxom blonde with pink highlights leaned back and crossed her arms across her chest.

Veronica turned to her. "I think we should have a dental health and wellness fair. One of our main strengths is the quality of services we offer, and I believe we should capitalize on that."

"A dental health and wellness fair?" Risha was the youngest member of the team and the dental assistant who sterilized equipment, prepared X-rays and teeth molds, and assisted Dr. Fuller and Veronica regularly. "I've never been to one. What's it like?"

"It's just like a regular health and wellness fair, but with a dental focus," Veronica replied. "We'll offer free dental examinations and education, and we'll invite some of our vendors to share their products and services, including insurance and financial payment plans. Each one will get a booth to set up in.

"If any patients end up needing further treatments, we'll offer them at discounted rates as long as they schedule them during the fair. They'd even get a chance to meet some of our specialists, who we'd ask to drop by for a limited time to answer questions and address any concerns they may have. Through the fair, we'll be leveraging a holistic dental approach, which I think would make an attractive value proposition to both new and existing patients."

"Sounds interesting," Risha said as she pushed her glasses up the bridge of her nose.

"It will be. Most clinics tend to schedule their preventive examinations right after New Year, but we'll get ahead of them. It's going to be a ton of work to set up though, and that's where I'll need your help."

"I'm all for it," Sheila said.

Veronica beamed. "Any questions before we dive into the details?" Angela and Risha both shook their heads. "Good. Now let me walk you through all we need to do."

For the next forty minutes, Veronica shared the details of her plan, and the team discussed each line item. By the time they were done, everyone understood the role they had to play and what they were responsible for. Sheila was tasked with making sure she brought Tami up to speed. Tami had been excused from the meeting to help prepare for the day's work at the clinic.

"I'm worried we won't be ready in time," Angela said. "Three weeks isn't long enough to have everything all set up."

"I admit it's going to be tight," Veronica said. "But I've already teased the ideas to a few company reps. They seem excited about it and are eager to come. We already have the venue we plan to use—Dr. Fuller reached out to his brother-in-law, and he's confirmed his hall's availability and locked it down for us. I know we have our normal daily workload to handle, but we can spend an extra hour each day to work on this project. Dr. Fuller has assured me he'll cover any overtime."

"We can do this, people," Sheila piped in. Veronica gave her a grateful smile.

"I'm in," Risha said. "Let's do this. What do you think, Angela?"

"Okay, I'm in too," Angela said. "Might as well rock the time before Christmas."

"Awesome." Veronica answered a few more questions, and then the meeting ended.

Everyone dispersed to get ready for the day's first appointments.

"I like what you've put together," Sheila said as she and Veronica headed to the door.

"Thank you," Veronica responded.

"I'm assuming we won't start the full marketing campaign across Dexington until we've locked down the vendors."

"Correct. But I believe it'll be easy to secure the vendors given how excited they are."

"I agree," Sheila said. They'd exited the conference room. "I'll see you later."

"Sure." She watched as Sheila returned to her office.

Veronica let out a long exhale. She'd been worried that the team would balk at the idea, but everything had worked out so far. Now she just needed to play her role and oversee all the moving parts.

And maybe, just maybe, she'd make Dr. Stone regret stepping on their clinic's toes.

CHAPTER 7

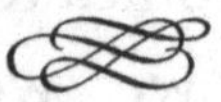

*V*eronica had just finished with her last patient for the day when Tami burst into her office.

"We have a problem," she said, her chest heaving as she fought to catch her breath.

"What is it?" Veronica asked as she finished up her patient notes on the computer and signed off. She hoped another patient hadn't collapsed in their waiting room. It had happened once, and they'd called nine-one-one and gotten the patient the care he needed before he had another stroke. Aside from a similar emergency, Veronica couldn't imagine what else could have had Tami all worked up.

"Toothy Grin has fliers everywhere promoting a dental fair just like ours."

Veronica's breath hitched. "Are you sure?"

Tami nodded. "I figured I'd run here and let you know ASAP."

Veronica could feel a headache coming on. They'd spent the past week preparing for their fair and had most of the vendors locked down. It'd been a joy working with the team to get it all set up. And they'd planned to start the marketing promotion tomorrow. Could this be a coincidence? Maybe not, but it could still work if they had theirs before Toothy Grin's. "Did you check when theirs is taking place?"

Tami grimaced. "Same day and time as ours."

Veronica's nostrils flared. Same date and time? Chances that this was a coincidence were almost nil.

"I called my cousin who works there to ask her about it," Tami continued. "She said they came up with the idea yesterday and decided to run with it."

Only yesterday? The news about Fuller's dental health fair must have leaked. "I want you to ask everyone to come to my office," Veronica said. Thankfully, Dr. Fuller had already left for the day—she had no idea how she would have explained what was happening to him.

A few minutes later, Sheila, Tami, Angela, and Risha were seated in her office. "I'm sure you've heard about Toothy Grin's dental fair," Veronica began. There were nods all around.

"Tami told us about it on our way in," Sheila said.

"Did anyone discuss the fair outside of this office?"

The room went silent. Veronica could have heard a pin drop. They'd all agreed they wouldn't talk about it until the marketing campaign started, so this was a big deal.

She ran a hand through her hair. "Please. I need to know. Did anyone mention anything?" Her eyes searched their faces, but everyone remained quiet.

Finally, Risha spoke up. "I'm sorry. I was so excited about what we had accomplished that I mentioned it to a friend in another state while waiting for Bus 90." Bus 90 was one of the buses that went to the suburbs.

"When was this?"

"Two days ago," Risha replied.

Veronica's heart fell. The news must have leaked. "Was anyone around you when you were holding this conversation?"

Risha shook her head. "I'm not sure. Wait! I remember someone wearing scrubs, a turquoise top with pink rubber ducky patterns, sitting on the bench. I thought at the time that the outfit was cute."

Tami gasped. "That top is Toothy Grin's uniform for the week! My cousin raved about it."

"Do you remember anything about her?" Veronica asked.

Risha thought for a moment. "She had a blonde bob with turquoise highlights. I remember liking that it matched her outfit." She wrung her hands together. "I'm so sorry."

Veronica pinched the bridge of her nose. This was the worst thing that could happen to them right now. "It's okay," she said.

But she couldn't help being angry at Toothy Grin. They'd stolen her patients, and now they were running with her idea. What thievery! There was no way she was going to let them get away with it.

"What do you plan to do now?" Sheila asked, a note of concern in her voice.

Veronica got up and grabbed her coat. "I believe it's time for a chat with their owner."

Veronica marched up to the front desk in Toothy Grin's spacious waiting room. The place was bright and airy, with colorful leather couches and seats interspersed throughout the space. She spotted two former patients of theirs lounging in the waiting room, but they averted their eyes in embarrassment. She didn't blame them—no patient was tied permanently to any dentist, though she would have appreciated some loyalty, given the wonderful care they'd received from Fuller Dental.

But they were not the reason Veronica was here. Thinking about her stolen idea had made her blood boil as she'd strode all the way to Toothy Grin, and she was practically seething by now.

"Welcome to Toothy Grin Dental," a young smart-looking lady said from behind the counter. A silk scarf with yellow ducky imprints was wrapped around her neck. "How may I help you today?"

Veronica forced herself to stay calm. "I'd like to see Dr. Stone," she said. "Tell him it's Dr. Brooks."

The receptionist's eyes darted in the direction of the hallway before returning to Veronica. "Dr. Stone is not available right now," she said. She hadn't even bothered picking up the phone to call him.

By now, Veronica was mad enough that smoke could have come out of her ears. So Dr. Stone was around but didn't want to see anyone. Well, she'd make him see her.

She turned and stalked off in the direction of the hallway.

"You can't go in there!" the receptionist called out in a panicked tone.

Veronica ignored her and searched for Dr. Stone's name on the doors that lined the hallway. She noticed a bulletin board on one of the walls between the offices and saw the promo flier in question hanging there. Veronica snatched it off the board and walked briskly as she continued to scan the names on the doors. Soon she had two more to check before she reached the end of the hallway. By now, the receptionist had almost reached her. Veronica had to find Dr. Stone's office before the lady caught up to her.

She checked the last one on the left. *Bingo!* She'd found it. She gave a quick knock and strode in before the occupant had a chance to respond.

Veronica screeched to a halt. The office was spacious with large floor-to-ceiling windows.

But the sight before her was the last thing she'd expected to see.

CHAPTER 8

*J*ude jerked as the door of his office slammed open. His staff knew better than to knock on his door once he'd signed off for the day. He'd just changed out of his scrubs behind the screen and had come back to his desk to pick up his cufflinks. Jude had been about to button up his shirt when the last person he'd expected to see barged into his office.

He swore under his breath. Jude had no hang-ups about his physique—he'd loved surfing while in California, so being shirtless was nothing new. But this was his office, and he deserved his privacy. He closed up his shirt quickly and tucked it into his pants. What was she even doing here? Her stalking was becoming ridiculous.

Veronica blushed and swallowed, her eyes flitting to his chest before darting back to meet his gaze. "I'm sorry," she muttered. "I didn't know. I'll just leave." She turned to go.

Was this some sick joke? Something she'd planned to trap him? The day had already been stressful enough, and Jude had had it at this point. "What are you doing here?" he asked in a cold voice. "Listen, lady, I don't appreciate being stalked. I'm going to have to file a restraining order if you come near me again."

She swirled back to face him, her eyes flashing. "Are you for real?" she said. She looked more furious by the moment. "Do I look like a stalker to you?"

The door opened, and Samantha, his receptionist, hurried in. "I'm sorry, Dr. Stone. I tried to stop her—"

"It's alright." He motioned for her to leave. He'd deal with this matter once and for all. Samantha shut the door behind her as she exited.

Jude turned back to Veronica. "If you're not a

stalker, why are you following me? This is the third time you've run into me in so many days."

She shook her head in disbelief. "Unbelievable. You must be crazy." She marched up to Jude like she was Joan of Arc. "First of all, you are the moron that forgot to leash his dog when running in a residential neighborhood. *You,*" she pointed a finger at him, "ran into me. Secondly, I wouldn't be here if you didn't steal my idea." She slammed the promo flier on the desk.

Jude picked up the flier. "This? We didn't steal your idea. This was a project suggested by one of my staff."

"Who conveniently stole the idea after eavesdropping on a member of my team at Fuller Dental."

Fuller Dental? He'd only discovered the place existed in his neighborhood after he'd bought his office building. It had been the only place for miles that fit his requirements and was available for sale. She was a dentist? *Crap.* Why did it feel like he'd just made a big mistake?

But Veronica had made a serious allegation against him. Considering what he'd gone through with the company he'd owned, Jude didn't tolerate stealing of any kind. He had to get to the bottom of this.

He tapped the speakerphone on his desk. "Could you please ask Lauren to come to my office? Thanks." He ended the call. "Please sit." He gestured to one of the visitors' chairs in his office.

Veronica folded her arms across her chest. "No thanks," she replied curtly. "I'd rather stand." She was definitely pissed, and somehow it seemed it was all his fault.

A minute later, Lauren walked in dressed in her scrubs. Jude had hired her to fill a dental assistant role last month, and so far she'd done a great job. "You asked for me, Dr. Stone?" Then her face blanched as soon as she spotted Veronica. What did that mean?

"Lauren, thanks for your idea about the dental fair. Could you tell me how you came up with it?"

Lauren bit her lower lip. "I…mmm…"

"Go on," Jude said. "I just need you to tell me the truth."

Lauren's forehead shone with sweat. "I overheard Dr. Brooks' staff talking about it on the phone, and I figured it was a great idea. I'm sorry."

Jude let out a small exhale. So Veronica had been right. "Lauren, you know we don't allow that here," he said in a quiet but firm voice.

Lauren refused to meet his eyes. "I'm sorry, Dr. Stone. I just wanted to impress you."

"You may return to work," Jude said. He'd have to deal with this matter later if he didn't want a repeat in the future. It was all his fault he hadn't probed to verify the source of the idea before taking it on. Instead, he'd ended up offending a colleague. He waited for Lauren to leave and then turned to Veronica. "My apologies, Dr. Brooks. I had no idea. We'll pull the project and put a stop to the promo."

Before Veronica could respond, the door burst open and a little boy with a mop of dark curly hair flew into his office. "Daddy!" He flung himself at Jude, who managed to catch him in time. "Will Santa Claus be at the fair? Yes? Yes?"

Jude hid a smile as he set him down on his feet and then bent to his son's eye level and tousled his hair. It had taken everything in him not to reject the suggestion of having Santa Claus at the fair. But seeing Caleb this way meant it had been worth it. "Caleb, Daddy has a visitor."

"Oops. Sorry!" he said in a quiet voice.

Jude turned him to face Veronica. "Dr. Brooks, this is my son, Caleb. Caleb, Dr. Brooks is a fellow dentist."

Caleb bent at the waist in a bow. "Nice to meet you, Dr. Brooks."

"Nice to meet you, Caleb," she responded and gave him a warm smile so bright that Jude blinked at its radiance. For one second, Jude wished the smile was for him instead.

Jude gave Caleb a nudge toward the door. "Caleb, could you play with Samantha for five minutes? I'll be right out."

"Okay." Caleb skipped to the door, opened it, and shut it quietly behind him.

"Sorry about that," Jude said to Veronica. "As I was saying, we'll cancel the promo and do whatever we can to make sure it doesn't affect your fair."

Veronica let out a sigh. "You don't have to."

Jude blinked. Did he hear right?

"The kid will be disappointed," Veronica said.

In that moment, Jude's regard for her grew a mile. She'd let go of her anger because of his kid? "You don't have to do that. He'll be fine."

"I'm sure he's not the only child looking forward to it if you're bringing Santa Claus. I'll look for another idea."

She'd done him a huge favor, one he wouldn't forget. "Thank you. My apologies once again, Dr. Brooks."

Veronica nodded and made her way toward the door to leave his office. As her hand rested upon the doorknob, she turned. "What was that about stalking?" she asked.

It was Jude's turn to be embarrassed, and his face and ears grew warm. "Let's just say I've had a stalking problem. But I'm sorry for misjudging you." He barely even thought before blurting out: "How about I make it up to you with lunch sometime?"

CHAPTER 9

*V*eronica stared at Dr. Stone like he'd grown two heads. Was he a psycho or something? One minute he'd called her a stalker, and now he was offering to take her out for lunch?

Definitely not happening. He was her enemy, and the loss of the idea stung even now. Sure, he'd apologized, but she had no second option yet to raise sales. Not to mention, she still needed to call her vendors, inform them the fair was no longer going to take place, and smooth things over with them. Most weren't going to be happy, and some of the relationships and goodwill Fuller Dental had cultivated over the years would be damaged.

Goodness gracious, she'd made things worse than before.

Her jaw tightened. "There's no need for that," Veronica responded. "Have a good day."

She turned and left the office. As she walked through the waiting room to exit the building, she could feel the receptionist's eyes on her, but Veronica ignored it.

More importantly, what was she going to do now?

Soon, Veronica was back in front of her clinic, and she trudged up the steps until she reached the doors and entered. Sheila came around as soon as she saw her. Veronica was surprised to see she'd waited for her. "What happened?" Sheila asked.

Veronica said nothing until she'd entered her office and sat down. The robin-blue walls with their colorful wall art of animals playing happily near water did nothing to calm her down. Sheila closed the door and took the opposite chair.

"It's too late," Veronica said. "We can't hold the dental fair anymore."

Shella's face turned solemn. "Did they steal the idea?"

Veronica nodded. "Yes, an employee stole the

idea, but the owner didn't know and offered to cancel their event."

"So why is it too late?"

"I couldn't do it. Let's just say I chose to be the bigger person here."

"So what do we do now?"

Veronica dropped her head into her hands. "I don't know, and we're running out of time. I thought about it all the way back, but no other ideas sprung to mind."

"Okay. Why don't we forget everything for now? It's Friday. Go home, enjoy your weekend, and let's come back on Monday with a fresh mind. We'll handle the vendors then. I'm also sure between all of us we can come up with a new idea, alright?"

Veronica said nothing and rubbed her forehead. She could feel a roaring headache coming on.

"Let's go." Sheila grabbed Veronica's bag and held it out to her.

Veronica accepted the bag and rose to her feet. Sheila was right. She needed to forget everything for now and blow off some steam. "Thanks, Sheila."

"You're welcome."

They left the office. By now, the rest of the practice had already shut down. Sheila and Veronica were the last to leave.

After Veronica had locked the entrance and made sure the security system was activated, they made their way down the steps and headed in the direction of the back lot where their cars were parked.

"So what did you think about him?" Sheila asked.

"Who?"

"Dr. Stone."

Veronica glanced at her. "Why?"

"He's cute."

Well, he was, but Veronica wasn't admitting that. "He's okay," she said instead.

"I'm pretty sure he's more than okay."

Veronica arched an eyebrow. "Sheila, aren't you supposed to be married?"

"Doesn't mean I don't have two good eyes to recognize a McDreamy when I see one."

Veronica chuckled. McDreamy was the last word she'd expected Sheila to use. How did she even know the word?

"Are you laughing at me?" Sheila asked in mock annoyance.

Veronica looped an arm through Sheila's. "You? Not possible. You're a sweetheart."

"That I am." At that, they both collapsed into laughter. "Alright, I won't talk about him anymore."

Veronica flashed her a warm smile. "Thank you."

She walked with Sheila to her car and waited until she'd left. Then Veronica headed to her car and peeled out of the parking lot. But the thoughts of what had happened lingered in her mind.

Now, how was she going to come up with a new idea that could be executed before Christmas?

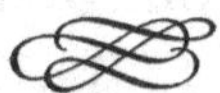

CHAPTER 10

Veronica woke the next day with a headache. It had receded last night but was now back in full force. She'd spent the rest of the evening at the mall picking up Christmas gifts for the kids at the orphanage and then passed the night thinking about what to do for the business. Veronica had tried to relax like Sheila had suggested, but her mind had remained restless. All the same, she hadn't been able to come up with any good ideas.

She jumped out of bed. Since staying in wasn't going to help her, she decided she might as well head to the orphanage. Veronica showered, dressed, and was out the door in fifteen minutes. She'd grab breakfast over there—there were always leftovers in the refrigerator.

By the time Veronica reached the orphanage, it was already mid-morning, and the sun was high in the sky. She parked in one of the available spaces in front of the building, bounded up the steps, and headed straight for the director's office to say hello.

Martha Stockbridge, St. Andrews Orphanage's director for as long as Veronica could recall, was like the mother she'd never had. Martha truly loved each child and was the main reason why many of the children had grown to be well-adjusted adults, Veronica included. Like Veronica, quite a number came back to help with the children or donated to make sure the kids had more than enough.

Veronica knocked at her door, but there was no response.

"She's not around," a familiar voice said.

Veronica turned to see Elise, the orphanage's cook and her close friend, carrying a tray of cookies. From the smell that emanated from it, Veronica was sure the cookies had just been retrieved from the large oven in the second kitchen that had been built at the back of the large house. "Hey, Elise," she said as she strode toward her.

"Keep your hands away from the cookies," the dark-haired beauty said with a smile. "They're spoken for."

"Just one. I'm sure it won't make a difference."

Elise hurried in the direction of the kitchen in the main house. "Your ones always end up being twos. I don't trust your fingers. Too sneaky."

Veronica managed to pilfer a cookie before Elise packed them up into a box. Then she settled against the large quartz kitchen counter as she nibbled the treat. "So where did Martha go?"

"She had breakfast with a sponsor. I'm sure she'll be back soon." Even though the Dexingtons, the first dwellers in the city and her best friend Sarah's family, supported the orphanage generously, Martha liked to touch base with the other sponsors whenever she could. "Every penny makes a difference" was her motto.

"So where are the kids?" The orphanage was unusually quiet. Veronica was surprised no one had followed the smell of cookies and pounced on them like she'd done.

"Sarah and Phillip have them over for the day at their estate. They bought some new horses, and the kids have gone to play with them. Geoffrey and Anna are there as well to help." Geoffrey was Phillip's butler, though he was super rich as well. "Only Johnny was left behind—he had a fever earlier but is much better now."

As if hearing his name, a seven-year-old boy with blond bangs, raced into the kitchen and then skidded to a stop. "Hey, Aunt Vee."

"Johnny!" Veronica pulled him into a hug. "I heard you had a fever." She placed her hand against his forehead—the temperature seemed normal. "Seems like you're much better now."

Johnny slipped out of her embrace—he'd never been a big hugger—and grinned up at her. "Well, I'll be much better if I had a few cookies."

Veronica let out a laugh. What do you know? The kid was smart.

Elise shook her head and hid a smile as she set a plate with two cookies and a glass of milk in front of him. "I can see you're milking it for all it's worth." Johnny wasted no time in scarfing the cookies down.

Elise glanced at Veronica. "How was your week? You look tired."

Veronica let out a sigh. "Just had a lot on my plate. I'm trying to come up with an idea for the clinic."

"Idea?" Johnny looked up from his snack, cookie crumbs at the corners of his mouth. "It's Christmas time!"

Christmas … an idea popped into Veronica's head, and she straightened from the counter. Excitement bubbled within her. Why hadn't she thought of that before? She grabbed Johnny and gave him a kiss on his forehead. "Thank you!"

Johnny blushed and tried to pretend it was nothing, but his chest was all puffed out.

"I'll see you later, Elise!" Veronica gave her a wave and practically ran to her car.

She had to get home fast to capture and crystallize the beginnings of a plan that was unfolding in her mind.

An idea that could change everything.

Veronica leaned back in her swivel chair and stretched her arms above her head.

Done. She'd been able to turn the idea into a proposal, detailing what could be achieved and what would be required and had sent it off to Dr. Fuller. She'd also explained what had happened to the previous project. Now all she needed was his go-ahead and she was good to go. But she was ninety-nine percent certain that he'd buy into the idea.

Veronica had remembered the twelve days of Christmas at the orphanage, and it had struck her that they could do something similar. Like five days of Christmas to thank and appreciate their patients. Sure, it wouldn't follow the traditional way of celebrating it, but that made it all the more fun.

For five days, at a certain time of the day, they would have different activities at the clinic targeted at kids. The back lot would be closed off and set up for games and fun activities, all of which would be dental-related in one form or the other. In addition, the clinic would hold a five-day giveaway event. Everyone who registered and underwent a free dental exam would get a chance to win a free procedure on the first day, one of two procedures on the second day, one of three procedures on the third day, etcetera. A list of five procedures would be provided each day for winners to choose from, and the winner for the day would be posted the next morning on the bulletin board in the waiting room. This meant patients would be incentivized to come back to the clinic to check the results, giving Veronica and her team another touch point with them.

All winners had to schedule their procedures within the next month and would be responsible for any prerequisites for more complex procedures. The final event would then end with a Christmas costume party on Saturday open to everyone, where every attendee had to dress up as a Christmas character or as a food that was good for the teeth.

Veronica believed the free dental exam would be a great way to get the word out about the clinic, give back to the community, and help identify new patients that needed additional dental work. Those who scheduled their procedures immediately would get discounts and more financial payment options available to them. The whole effort would require some nifty planning to get it all ready within a week, but Veronica was sure her team was up for it.

Her computer pinged with the arrival of a new email, and Veronica opened it. *Yes!* Dr. Fuller was on board and had even added a few ideas of his own that made the event better. Dr. Fuller's wife was also a retired middle school teacher and had volunteered to come with a few of her former colleagues to help supervise the kids each day.

Veronica smiled to herself. This idea was way more fun than the other one she'd given up. Hopefully, the event would work out and help the clinic raise revenue that would help mitigate their losses from the previous months after Toothy Grin had opened their business.

Her mind went to Dr. Stone for a moment, and Veronica finally let herself think about what had happened yesterday in his office. Dr. Stone had looked really good in his button-down shirt. The abs of steel she'd glimpsed had been perfect just like she'd expected. Veronica liked a man who stayed fit.

But she'd been surprised he had a son. Did that mean there was a woman or wife in the picture? Veronica longed for a good relationship, but a man-snatcher or cheater she was not. Even though she wasn't admitting she would have loved to date him, Dr. Stone was now definitely out of the running.

Veronica let out a long exhale. It was best she forgot about him and focused on saving her business.

Veronica paced her office as the warm afternoon sun filtered in through the windows. It had been a long week juggling her patient load and prepping for the event, which she'd scheduled a week before Dr. Stone's, but she and her team had done it.

The team had promoted the event across the surrounding neighborhoods and even in downtown Dexington. Dr. Fuller's teenage niece and her friends had gone door-to-door sharing fliers about the event, and Veronica's team had also pounded the pavement as well once they were done with their daily appointments.

Veronica had set up social media ads that targeted their neighborhood, and their contracted website manager had worked his

SEO magic to the point that searching "dental" and "Dexington" online brought up their event on the first page. Their current patients had also been encouraged to share the news by word-of-mouth. Sheila had even brought in contractors after hours to work on the offices and waiting room, and together with Veronica, they'd given the spaces a much-needed facelift.

Everything else was in place, and the event was expected to start next week.

But Veronica was nervous.

She hoped all their efforts had been enough, yet a doubt that they might not succeed lingered.

A knock sounded on her door, and Veronica halted. "Come in," she said.

Sheila entered clad in a pink blouse and black slacks. "This just came for you." She extended an envelope to Veronica.

Veronica accepted the gold envelope and opened it. She pulled out the gold-embossed card inside. It was a personal invitation from Dr. Stone for Dr. Brooks to attend their fair as a special guest.

"What is it?" Sheila asked.

Veronica looked up and caught her gaze.

"Dr. Stone would like me to attend their fair as a special guest."

"Are you going to go?"

Veronica re-inserted the card into the envelope and placed it on her desk. "I don't think so."

"It seems like he's extending an olive branch to you. Maybe consider going? I'm sure he was able to pull in more vendors to attend the event. It might be a good place for you to expand your industry connections."

What Sheila said made sense, though Veronica would have liked nothing better than to stay away from Dr. Stone. Of course, it didn't have anything to do with the fact that her emotions might get all confused if she saw him again. "I'll think about it. Right now, I'm more worried about our event. I'm hoping it'll go well."

"I'm sure it'll work out just fine," Sheila said before turning and leaving Veronica's office.

Veronica prayed she was right.

CHAPTER 11

The week had been a success, much more than Veronica had anticipated. It seemed she had fretted for nothing. They'd been jammed with loads of new patients, and Veronica's schedule for the next three months was fully booked. It was truly God's blessing.

They'd gotten such a positive response from the local community for the Christmas party that they'd had to move the venue from the top floor of their office to the large restaurant owned by Dr. Fuller's brother-in-law two streets away. The party was expected to start by four pm. The team had worked all morning with volunteers to set up the place, and the restaurant staff had prepped all the food and drinks.

All that was left now was for Veronica to change for the party. She'd brought her outfit to the office and now shimmied into the snowman dress she'd bought online. Since guests were expected to dress up as Christmas characters or as dental-enriching food, Veronica had chosen a white A-line knee-length dress with large, black decorative buttons running down the center and a wide black belt looped at its waist. She completed her get-up with green and red striped stockings, a green and red scarf around her neck, and a mini black top hat she'd decorated with fake carrot spikes. She might as well get her vegetables in somehow.

Veronica studied herself in the full-length mirror in the bathroom. She looked good if she said so herself. Once she'd finished her light makeup and was satisfied with her appearance, she donned her coat, locked the office, and set off on foot in the direction of the restaurant. Everyone else from her team was already there, and Sheila had called to let her know that the guests had started arriving.

The trees that lined her pathway were now skeletal with blankets of fallen rust- and gold-colored leaves at their bases. Yet they sparkled with the Christmas light decorations that had been put up this week on them. A gentle cool breeze skirted the air, and Veronica inhaled deeply. The sun had begun to lower in the horizon, painting the sky with hues of orange, purple, and crimson.

Then Veronica felt a prickling sensation at the back of her neck as soon as she turned onto the street that led to the restaurant. She whirled around but saw no one behind her and nothing out of the ordinary. What could it be?

Veronica resumed her walk. By now, there were only a few people on the street, though cars zoomed by on their way to and from the suburbs.

But the feeling persisted, and the hairs on her neck stood up.

Veronica's heart thudded in her chest. Maybe it was her imagination, but she heard faint footfalls that seemed to try to match hers. She quickened her steps, not bothering to look behind her. It was more important than ever to reach her destination.

The steps behind her picked up as well.

Veronica's pulsed raced. Now, she was

convinced someone was tailing her. She stared straight ahead. Just one more block and she'd be at the restaurant. She hurried onwards, the lights from the restaurant flashing like a beacon to her. Veronica was grateful she'd gone with her trusty, black pumps instead of the strappy high-heels she'd planned to wear before.

She soon reached the restaurant and let out a sigh of relief as soon as she saw Sheila standing in front of the entrance and waving her over. Veronica glanced behind her, but there was no one there, and the footfalls had stopped.

"Is everything alright?" Sheila asked.

The prickling sensation was no more, like it'd never happened in the first place. Veronica turned back and flashed Sheila a warm smile. "Yes." She linked her arm with Sheila's. "Now, let's go inside and have a great party," she said and led the way in.

But what had that been all about?

Veronica wove her way through the party until she reached a quiet area of the room. The restaurant was made up of a larger space that then narrowed into a smaller room. The team had set up kid-friendly booths in the candy-cane-themed smaller space, and a quick peek in showed the kids were having a blast all dressed in colorful costumes.

She didn't think there was any 'vegetable' missing as far as she could tell, and one child was even dressed as a giant set of pink gum and white teeth. A number of kids ran around with painted designs on their faces. An adult volunteer stayed on a chair by the entrance to ensure the kids only left their area when escorted by an adult with a matching bracelet to theirs.

The adults stayed in the larger space, and the sound of chatter and laughter filled the room. The team had done a great job in sprucing up the place, and now Christmas lights twinkled overhead in straight lines from one end of the ceiling to the other. Green, red, and gold Christmas balls dropped low from the ceiling, while small holiday wreaths hung like paintings on the wall at intervals around the restaurant.

A hot cocoa stand stood like a sentry by the entrance to the kids' area. It was manned by one of the restaurant staff who served hot cocoa floats with marshmallows and green and red peppermint sprinkles, a favorite it seemed for the kids. Waiting staff passed among guests, serving wreath-style-plated hors d'oeuvres and glasses of virgin jingle juice and sparkling cranberry punch.

"Hello, Doctor," a child-like voice said. Veronica glanced down to see a boy with black curly hair wearing a carrot outfit. She looked closer, and her eyes widened. It was the boy she'd met in Dr. Stone's office, his son. What was his name again? Yes, Caleb. But what was he doing here? Did it mean…?

Sure enough, his father strode toward her, his long legs eating up the distance between them. "Hello, Dr. Brooks," he said as soon as he reached her. And just like that, Veronica felt a warm tingle coil up within her at the sound of his voice.

This is so embarrassing, she chided herself. She had no reason to feel this way around him. In fact, she was just going to ignore the feeling and pretend it hadn't happened. Nothing good could come from acknowledging it. "Hello, Dr.

Stone," she said with a smile. "What are you doing here?"

"I heard the whole neighborhood was invited, Caleb wanted to come, and so here we are. It seems like a great party."

"It is. Thank you. What about your wife?" It was a sneaky way to confirm the truth.

Caleb motioned for Veronica to bend. She did and lent him her ear. "Oh, Daddy is not married," he whispered. "Would you like to be daddy's girlfriend?"

Veronica fought to hide her shock and felt her face warm up. This kid was bold. But he'd done her a solid and confirmed Dr. Stone's marital status. His expectant face looked up at her, waiting for her response. But what could she say?

Instead, Veronica gave him a warm smile and tweaked his nose. Caleb grinned in response.

"What did you ask the good doctor?" Dr. Stone said.

"Nothing," Veronica replied. "It's a secret." There was no way she was letting him know what had just transpired. Caleb nodded vigorously in agreement.

Dr. Stone ruffled his son's hair. "So you're keeping secrets from me now?" he said with a mock frown. Caleb stuck out his tongue at him and then ran off into the kids' area. Dr. Stone watched him leave with a smile on his face.

Veronica's heart skipped a beat at the brilliance of his smile. Gosh, even his profile was so handsome. And he was still single? It was a little hard to believe. And why? Was he a horrible person, a wolf in sheep clothing? Maybe, but she didn't think so—Caleb looked like a well-adjusted child from a happy home, even if she didn't know anything about his father.

But Veronica couldn't trust her heart on it. She'd been wrong before, else why would she have ended up in relationships with two douchebags who'd both dumped her during Christmas?

She clamped the thoughts down. What was wrong with her? She had a party to preside over and guests to take care of instead of standing here dreaming about a man that was supposed to be her enemy.

"It was nice seeing you, Dr. Stone," Veronica said. From the corner of her eye, she spotted the parent of a patient she needed to catch up with coming into the restaurant. "I need to attend to my other guests. But please stay and enjoy the party." Veronica didn't wait for his response and took off toward her guest.

It was best to create as much distance as possible between Dr. Stone and her.

Jude watched Veronica leave yet again. It seemed this was her way, but one of these days he'd make sure he got a chance to sit down with her and get to know her better.

Because she intrigued him.

He'd been surprised when she'd given up her project, though he'd been a bit disappointed when she hadn't responded to the invitation he'd sent. His messenger had assured him he'd delivered the card to her office.

Somehow, Jude couldn't get Veronica out of his mind. He'd made sure to look her up. it'd turned out she was a well-known pediatric dentist and seemed to care very much about the children at a certain St. Andrews orphanage—Jude had seen multiple photographs of her with them at various charitable events. It seemed she didn't fit into either the gold digger or the stalker category. The knowledge had only made him more curious about her.

Something about Veronica tugged at the recesses of his memories, but Jude couldn't figure out what. So when Caleb had stated his interest in attending the party, Jude had tagged along instead of sending his mother with Caleb like he'd done for every other Christmas party they'd ever been invited to. Of course, he'd justified it with the excuse that he only wanted to come and meet more members of the community, but his heart knew better.

"How are you doing today, Dr. Stone?" Jude turned to see the petite lady with the silver bob who he'd seen before with Veronica.

"I'm doing great, Ms. …"

"It's Sheila."

"Nice to meet you, Ms. Sheila." The hand that shook his was firm, unlike what he'd expected for a woman of her age.

"I hope you're enjoying the party," she said.

"It looks great," he replied politely. The

Christmassy vibe of the party still got to him, but he was learning to ignore it.

"Are you married, Dr. Stone?" she asked with a deadpan look on her face.

Well, his marital status wasn't a secret—Jude had even been named one of the top hundred eligible bachelors in California. "I'm single," he replied.

"A bachelor. Nice."

He could see the gears of her mind turning, and Jude was willing to pay more than a penny for her thoughts.

"Would you like some shrimp?" she asked. A waiter had stopped by where they stood and now offered them grilled shrimp on a skewer.

Jude accepted one and took a bite. It was delicious. "This tastes really good," he said.

"Yes, it does," Sheila replied. "So what do you think of Dr. Brooks?"

Woah! Where did that come from? Ms. Sheila was definitely a straight shooter. Jude tried to read her, but her face remained inscrutable.

He had to tread carefully here. Was she trying to matchmake them? It was interesting to realize he wasn't opposed to the idea. "I haven't had a chance to really get to know her, but I think she's great from what I see. She threw this wonderful party, didn't she?" he said in a noncommittal voice.

"Yes she did. Okay, I need you to do something for me," she said.

"What is it?"

She led him to a corner of the room, where a large Christmas tree that had been tastefully decorated stood. "Could you wait here for me? I'll be right back." She didn't give him a chance to respond before she got lost in the crowd.

Now what was Ms. Sheila up to? Yet Jude obeyed and waited. In fact, the location gave him a vantage point to see what was going on in the rest of the room.

Soon he saw Sheila leading Veronica to where he stood, a look of confusion on her face. *Well, that makes two of us*, he thought to himself.

Soon Veronica was standing in front of him. "What's going on, Sheila?" she asked.

"Look up," Sheila commanded.

Jude glanced up, and what he saw made him freeze. For goodness sake, why hadn't he noticed? Veronica's eyes widened in shock.

"You may kiss now," Sheila said with a mischievous grin.

Veronica couldn't believe what she was seeing. When had those sprigs of mistletoe ended up on the crown molding? They hadn't been there when she'd left to change for the party. She shot a fierce glance at Sheila, only to see a satisfied smile on her face.

It must have been intentional. But how had Sheila known that Dr. Stone would be here this evening? Or was this a prank she'd planned for any unsuspecting parties? She was pretty certain Sheila would never tell her.

She glanced at Dr. Stone. He seemed just as bewildered as she was.

"Kiss. Kiss," Sheila had started up the chant.

Soon all eyes in the room turned to them, and others joined in.

I'm going to kill you, Veronica mouthed to Sheila, but she only laughed and instead increased the speed of her chant a notch. "Kiss. Kiss."

No way was Veronica going to do it, even if she now knew the hot doctor was single. Dr. Stone was practically a stranger and an enemy to boot. The best way out was just to walk away as fast as possible and hope the humiliation would be forgotten shortly. Yes, an escape to the bathroom sounded really good right now. She'd go there and probably never come out until the party was over.

Veronica had only taken a step when she felt an arm wrap around her waist and draw her close to a solid, muscled frame.

She shot Dr. Stone a panicked look. What was he doing?

His warm minty breath caressed her cheek, and Veronica fought the urge to inhale it. As those beautiful brown eyes searched hers, Veronica felt herself grow calm under his gaze.

He must have seen what he was looking for

because he lowered his mouth to hers and kissed her.

It was like all the nerve endings in her body came alive in that moment. Everything else faded away—the shouts, clapping, whistling—and suddenly, it was like they were the only two people in the room. Veronica had no idea a man's lips could taste this good—it was a mixture of sweetness, mint, and spice.

And she wanted more.

She wrapped her arms around his neck and pulled him closer. It seemed it was all the invitation Dr. Stone needed before he dove in and kissed her like she was the oxygen he needed. Stars exploded behind Veronica's eyes, and the butterflies in her stomach clamored for attention. By the time he broke the kiss, Veronica had gone to heaven and back.

Dr. Stone planted a final gentle kiss on her forehead to allow her to catch her breath, and then he released her.

It took a minute for Veronica to be steady on her feet again. *Wow!* The kiss was the last thing she'd expected, but she had to admit that she'd liked it. A lot.

Hold on! What had she just done? Veronica had kissed another doctor right in front of some of her patients, and everyone had witnessed it. Now all the guests would think they were an item when in reality they were not. She fought the urge to cover her face. "I have to go," she said.

Veronica left him standing there and hurried in the direction of the bathroom while avoiding eye contact with anyone. The pale yellow and white space was empty, and Veronica locked herself in one of the stalls. She took big gulps of air as she slumped against its door.

She started when she heard a knock on the door. "Are you alright?" It was Sheila, a note of concern in her voice.

"I'm fine. I just need a minute."

Sheila hesitated before responding. "Okay." Soon the sound of her footsteps faded as she walked away and exited the bathroom.

Veronica exhaled. *You have to pull yourself together*, she thought to herself. Kiss or no kiss, she still had a party to finish.

She stayed a few minutes to gather herself. Then Veronica unlocked the door and washed her hands. Taking a deep breath to steady herself, she squared her shoulders and left the bathroom.

Her eyes instinctively searched the room, but Dr. Stone was nowhere to be seen. Fighting the urge to go look for him, she spent the rest of the evening in the kids' area, enjoying their fun and games. The children even watched a short Christmas movie, and Santa Claus entertained them by reading Christmas stories. Even though the children made her laugh with their antics, Veronica couldn't forget what had happened earlier. But soon enough, she had to thank the guests for coming, and the party came to an end.

Veronica couldn't recall how she managed to wrap up the party, pick up her things from the office, and arrive safely home. As she settled into bed after washing up, all her mind wanted to do was dwell on the kiss: the feel of his arms around her and, oh, those soft lips.

But this was as far as it would ever go.

The kiss had been a mistake, though a sweet one. It was best to remember that every time she'd gotten involved with someone, he'd only ended up breaking her heart during the Christmas season. And she was right in the middle of one. She couldn't afford to make the same misstep again.

Since they'd managed to avert the crisis with the dental practice in the short-term, all Veronica needed to do now was enjoy the rest of the season without having her heart broken, rest well, come up with a plan for the long-term, and then face the coming year with all the energy and vigor she had.

There was no space on her schedule for a relationship.

This was where it was going to end.

Even if Dr. Stone was uppermost on her mind as she drifted off to sleep.

CHAPTER 14

Jude stood by the floor-to-ceiling windows of his study and stared out at the twinkling stars covering the dark velvet sky. It was one of the reasons he'd moved into this area of town, where the beauty of the outdoors was still preserved. But that wasn't what occupied his mind as sleep fled his eyes.

Caleb had zonked out in the car on the way home, and Jude had taken him straight to bed after removing his costume and cleaning him up. The rest of the household was already fast asleep, but for some reason, Jude couldn't do the same.

Because of the kiss.

Jude couldn't believe he'd gone for it. He'd been shocked when Sheila had set them up. But as Veronica had made to walk away, a part of him had wanted the kiss. He guessed he'd wanted to know if Veronica was affected by him, as he was by her.

Because yes, Jude was interested in her.

As much as he hadn't wanted to believe it, there was something about her he couldn't seem to turn away from. Of course he wasn't saying he was in love—Jude had no plans to open himself up to anyone like that. The times he'd been hurt in the past were more than enough for a lifetime. But he couldn't resist the desire to get to know her and understand what made her tick. That wasn't such a big deal, right?

But she'd walked away from him after the kiss. Jude had thought she'd enjoyed it from the way she'd wrapped her arms around his neck and reciprocated, but it appeared he'd been wrong. Veronica had rushed to the bathroom and hadn't come back for a while. And when she finally did, she'd made a beeline for the kids' area without looking for him. To her, it was like the kiss had meant nothing. Come to think of it, how could he have thought she was a stalker when she was always in a hurry to get away from him?

So Jude had made an effort to avoid her for the rest of the night. It was her party after all, and the last thing he'd wanted was to make things uncomfortable for her.

Of course it had hurt his ego, but that was the risk he'd taken. It had become apparent as the night went on that she wanted nothing to do with him, and Jude was going to respect her wishes.

Maybe it was better this way. She wouldn't have to expect more from him than he could offer, and it was also possible they could have hated each other.

For now, Jude needed to get his head in the game and focus on getting through his first real Christmas in a long time, while spending quality time with his son and mom.

Just thinking about Caleb made Jude's heart swell with happiness. He remembered when he'd first encountered Caleb at one of the free dental clinics Jude had liked to organize. The boy had been abandoned by his family because of his maxillofacial malformations and had ended up in foster care. But you would never have known from the way he'd grinned at Jude when they'd met for the first time. In that moment, Jude had seen a replica of himself in Caleb, and he'd known he would adopt him. His friends and colleagues had kicked against the idea since he was single, but Jude's mind had been made up. If a lady didn't want to be in his life because he had a son, then so be it.

Jude had called in favors and pulled strings to fast-track the adoption process and made sure Caleb got out of the foster home that had been slowly killing him as soon as possible. He'd cared for Caleb through those first few months when he'd woken up daily with nightmares and had gotten a first-hand crash course on what it meant to be a father. Jude had held Caleb's hand all through the multiple surgeries he'd needed to correct the malformation, something Jude's father had never done.

And it had been worth it. Many people thought Caleb was lucky to have Jude as a father, but it was the other way round. Caleb had brought so much joy, laughter, and sunshine into Jude's life that he couldn't imagine how he'd survived without it before.

But Caleb tended to keep strangers at bay.

He'd avoided all the women that had shown an interest in Jude. In fact, Jude suspected Caleb had had a hand in driving some of them away.

So imagine his surprise when Caleb had taken to Veronica. He'd even shared a secret with her that Jude wasn't privy to!

He chuckled at the memory as he folded his arms across his chest. This was yet another reason why Jude had been curious about Veronica. Something about her must have made Caleb feel comfortable around her, and this was huge as far as Jude was concerned.

But he had to forget all that since Veronica didn't seem to care for him.

Jude was a big boy and would get over it—his life was fine the way it was and would always be.

Now, all he had to do was treat Veronica like the respected colleague she was, without expecting anything more.

Even though his heart ached at the thought of it.

CHAPTER 15

The week after the Christmas party had been busy for Veronica as the Fuller Dental team wrapped up its work for the year and shut down for the holidays. The clinic was closed from the week before Christmas until after the New Year. Emergency contact information had been sent out to patients via email. Veronica hoped that by next year they'd have an automated text messaging system that would send out alerts like this to all patients. As was custom for the team at the end of the year, they were having a final lunch together. This time, it was at a traditional Korean restaurant.

Dr. Fuller was the only one absent—he'd

gotten a last-minute call from one of their elderly dental patients who'd needed a quick follow-up at home after a procedure. It was a service that Dr. Fuller liked to offer patients who were frail in health and couldn't make it to the clinic as often as needed.

The restaurant had just opened a few months ago, and the food was delicious. Veronica had ordered the traditional Korean ox bone soup, *seolleongtang*, simmered on low heat for hours and containing light noodles, slices of beef, and green onions. She had chosen to add some pepper to give it some kick, and she now found herself with a satiated belly full of warm food.

Sheila had opted for a hotpot of mixed rice, *dolsot bibimbap*, a fusion of rice at the bottom with sauteed vegetables, an egg, toasted seaweed flakes, and sesame seeds at the top, all served in a hot earthenware pot. Sheila didn't speak to anyone throughout the meal, a sure sign the food had hit the right spots.

Dessert was a sweet gooey deep fried snack and tofu cream tiramisu. By the time they were done, Veronica was so stuffed all she wanted to do was take a nap.

"Ah, this was so good," Angela said. "I'm glad we came here today. I think I see myself returning here with Sean." Sean, her husband was a foodie. This place would probably be like heaven for him.

"So what are you all doing for Christmas?" Risha asked.

"Tons of relaxation and thinking about nothing except stuffing my face with Christmas treats," Veronica said.

"You're so lucky it doesn't show on you, Dr. Brooks," Tami said. "If I tried the same, I'm sure I'd probably gain ten pounds." Veronica had been blessed with a high metabolism, and she was grateful for it.

"Now that we've filled our tummies, I think we can talk about the elephant in the room," Angela said.

What was Angela talking about? Veronica thought they'd had great camaraderie all day.

"Yes, we need to talk about the kiss," Sheila said with a twinkle in her eye.

What kiss? Wait, they didn't mean …

"That kiss was hot, Dr. Brooks," Risha said.

"So electrifying that there were sparks in the

air," Sheila said. "Remember, I had a front row seat to the whole thing."

"I still plan to get back at you for that setup," Veronica promised.

"Really? After you were practically gobbling up that tall order of ice cream?" The other girls chuckled.

Veronica shook her head in disbelief. "Are you ladies serious right now?"

"As serious as a root canal," Angela said. Everyone burst out in laughter, including Veronica. It was hard to take Angela seriously sometimes.

"Really you guys looked great together," Angela continued. "Should we be expecting wedding bells soon? I'm assuming the hatchet between you two has been buried by the looks of that kiss."

"Will you be attending his fair tomorrow?" Tami chimed in. Veronica was assuming she'd heard about the invitation from Sheila.

"No, I don't plan to attend," Veronica said. "And there's nothing going on between us. It was just a mistletoe kiss. I'm not interested in a relationship with him."

"Keep telling yourself that," Sheila muttered.

"What? I see how you look at him and him at you. You were practically searching for each other for the rest of the party."

Veronica's face grew warm. "Sheila!"

"It's God's own truth," Sheila replied. She let out a sigh. "Veronica, I really think he's a good one for you, and I'd hate for you to miss him without even taking the chance to find out if he's the one."

But Veronica didn't want to dwell on anything related to Dr. Stone, at least not now. She reached out her hand and covered Sheila's. "Thanks for the advice, O Sage One, but can we talk about something else?"

They switched topics and chatted about the new theater that was opening up in the neighborhood next week in time for Christmas. Then they exchanged the gifts they'd bought for each other. Veronica ended up with a scarf from Sheila, a set of the ballpoint pens she liked to use from Angela, a ladybug mini desktop vacuum from Risha, and a beautiful cactus from Tami.

Veronica had given them each a premium spa package at the high-end Waterbridge Mall. She'd gone there once with Sarah, and the spa treatment had been heavenly. Everyone was excited about their gifts, but Veronica couldn't shut out Sheila's words—they kept ringing over and over again in her ears.

Maybe it was time she sought additional advice.

CHAPTER 16

*V*eronica called Sarah as soon as she got home in the evening. Sarah had been her best friend since high school, though they'd lost contact when Sarah's parents had moved to California without notice. They'd reconnected a few years ago before Sarah returned to Dexington for Christmas, met the love of her life—one of Dexington's "royalty"—and got married. Now she had a one-year-old son, Blake, and was as happy as ever.

"Hi, Sarah," Veronica said as she settled into the plush, cuddle-worthy green and red throw pillows on her couch. She loved to redecorate her apartment to match the seasons, so her living room was awash in colors of red, green, and gold.

"Hey, you," Sarah responded in a cheerful voice.

Veronica could hear some banging in the background. "What's going on?"

"It's Blake. He's discovered the toy drum set his grandma sent from California and has been banging it ever since."

"That must be fun."

"Fun? Try hearing that constantly for hours at a time. I feel like my eardrums might burst anytime soon."

"But he's such a cutie."

"That's his saving grace," Sarah responded like a proud mama.

"So when did you get back? How was the wedding?" Sarah had traveled out-of-town for her mom's wedding. Her mom had gotten remarried after Sarah's father had left and divorced her many years ago.

"Last night. It was great. Neil is a good guy for her."

"I'm glad she's happy."

"She is. I heard your event was great. Congrats!"

"Thanks. It worked out better than I'd expected."

"So what's going on with you?" Sarah asked.

"What do you mean?" Veronica said.

"I can tell from the sound of your voice that something's bothering your mind. Does it have anything to do with a certain mistletoe kiss? Spill."

Veronica groaned. "You heard about that too?"

Sarah chuckled. "You're very popular, my friend. Someone told me she took notes as she watched you guys."

"Oh shoot me already."

Sarah laughed. "You know it's a compliment, right?"

Veronica straightened. "There's nothing between Dr. Stone and me!"

"If you say so."

Veronica collapsed back on the couch. Why didn't anyone believe her? "I'm serious!"

Sarah chuckled. "Listen, Veronica. There's nothing wrong with finding a young, single man like Dr. Stone attractive. Besides, I'd like to be an aunt soon."

"You're crazy, you know that, right? Aren't

you satisfied after popping Blake out? Besides, Geoffrey has a newborn you can love on."

"True. But you can never have too many nieces or nephews. But what is it about Dr. Stone that's bugging you?"

"It's not him per se."

"So you like him." Sarah's voice had turned serious.

"I don't know. Sure, I think he's attractive. But you know what's up with me and relationships during the Christmas season. It's too risky. And after the issue with work, I really just want to enjoy Christmas with no further mishaps."

"Listen, Vee. You can't allow fear to rule your life. Sometimes you just need to take a step of faith and see where it goes. Remember, I thought Phillip and I would never match, but it's one of the best decisions I ever made, and I would have made a mistake and missed him if you hadn't encouraged me. So now I'm doing the same for you. Vee, give love a chance. If it's not him, then you know you've tried your best. And who says it won't be different this time around?"

Sarah had been blessed to meet a man like Phillip who was down-to-earth despite how much money he had. Veronica had learned to stay as far away as possible from men with lots of money after her ex-fiancé had used it and the fact that she'd grown up in an orphanage as reasons to disparage her and break up the relationship. Thankfully, she didn't think it applied to Dr. Stone. "But I don't really know him."

"Then take the time and do that. Find out what kind of man he is. Why don't you start by attending his event? You'll get a chance to see how he interacts with people there."

Veronica sat up. "How do you know about that? Sarah, do you have a spy in my office?"

Sarah chuckled from the other end of the line. "Let's just say I know a lot of things. So, put your feelings aside and go. The worst that can happen is that you'll make new connections in the industry."

"Okay. I'll consider it."

"That's my girl." A loud cry split the air. "I have to go. It looks like Blake is hungry. You know how he gets when he doesn't get his food immediately. Helen says Phillip was the same at his age." Helen was Phillip's mother and Sarah's mother-in-law.

"Thanks, dear, for the pep talk."

"You're welcome. Any time. Talk to you later. Bye."

"Bye." The line went dead.

Veronica dropped the phone beside her and let her head fall back against the couch. Everything Sarah had said made sense. Maybe things could be different with Dr. Stone—she'd never know unless she gave what she'd felt between them at the party a chance. Besides, Veronica had nothing to lose and everything to gain by attending the dental fair.

What harm could it possibly do?

CHAPTER 17

*V*eronica had planned to make an appearance at the dental fair on time, but her plans got derailed by a dental emergency she needed to take care of. By the time she was done seeing the seven-year-old, who'd suffered multiple dental trauma and whose permanent teeth had been knocked out, it was already evening. She considered missing the fair but figured it was better attending late than never.

Toothy Grin's office lobby was already buzzing by the time Veronica arrived. She noticed a young man in his early thirties wearing a headset and assumed he must know where she had to go.

"Hello," Veronica said as she approached him.

"Good evening," he replied with a warm smile. "How may I help you?"

"Do you know how I can get to the dental fair? I'm looking for Dr. Stone." Since he'd invited her as a special guest, Veronica had decided to connect with him first.

"And you are?"

"Dr. Brooks." She showed him the invitation card.

"I'll take you to him," the young man said in a polite tone. "Please follow me."

The man led her to a set of elevators a few feet away. Soon they arrived on the third floor of the building. They passed through a set of large glass doors, and then they were right in the middle of the fair.

"Please wait here," the man said. "I'll be right back."

He disappeared into the crowd, and Veronica took the opportunity to look around. The entire floor had been dedicated to the fair. The space was packed, and people waited in lines near booths that had been set up in various sections of the large room—not what she'd expected at a time when the event should have been winding down. Veronica saw vendors she recognized and others she'd only heard of but never spoken with.

She felt a prickling feeling on the back of her neck. Veronica turned, but there were so many unfamiliar faces she wasn't sure what she was looking for. *Maybe it's just my imagination,* she thought. She turned back to the vendors she'd been studying.

Then Veronica felt the hairs on her skin rise. Her heart thudded, and she swiveled to see what or who it was that was eliciting the reaction. This time, there was no-one behind her. What was going on?

The man returned with Dr. Stone by his side, and Veronica forgot what had just happened. Dr. Stone looked so good in a pair of grey pants and a light blue button-down shirt, and his face seemed to light up when he saw her.

"Hello, Dr. Brooks," he said in that voice that turned her insides to mush. "I'm glad you could join us."

"Thanks for inviting me," Veronica said.

Dr. Stone gestured to the man beside him. "I assume you've met my executive assistant and right-hand man, Tyler. He's the one who made all this organizational magic happen."

"It's nice to meet you, Dr. Brooks," Tyler said. He listened to something coming through the headset. "I'm sorry. I have to go." He flashed her a smile. "I hope I get a chance to see you again."

"That'd be great," Veronica responded with a smile of her own. There was something easygoing and approachable about Tyler that endeared her to him.

He gave her a quick nod and left, already giving out orders in response to whatever he'd heard.

"Why don't I show you around?" Dr. Stone said.

"Sure." Veronica remembered then what had happened earlier, and the feeling of uneasiness returned. She turned to look behind her again, but saw nothing out of the ordinary.

Maybe it was just a fluke and nothing to worry about. So she ignored the disquiet that prickled at the pit of her stomach and instead allowed Dr. Stone to lead the way.

They started at one end of the fair and slowly made their way through from vendor to vendor.

Some were from dental companies, while others were specialists that complemented Toothy Grin's work. Veronica chatted enthusiastically with the ones she already knew and followed Dr. Stone's lead for the ones she didn't. A few shared their new ideas. Others seemed surprised to see them together, but Dr. Stone made it seem like it was something to be expected since their clinics were in the same zip code.

After a while, Dr. Stone asked her if she would like a break, but Veronica insisted they continue. She wanted to cover all the vendors before the event ended. They carried on for yet another hour, keeping the interruption brief with vendors that had lines of people waiting and chatting more extensively with those who didn't have one.

But most of all, Veronica had a chance to see both the funny and serious sides of Jude. He was charming without being annoying to the vendors and patients. Veronica could easily tell which vendors he had long-term relationships with—he tended to laugh and joke more with those. A few even commented that they looked great together. But it was apparent he valued his vendors and had good partnerships with them.

Veronica loved that Dr. Stone presented her to them like a valued partner of his, expecting them to accord her the same level of respect they'd given him. He listened carefully to whatever she had to say, and their discussions ended up both enlightening and entertaining. This was refreshing—Veronica had met all kinds of people in her line of work, and a few still stuck to the antiquated way of doing business, by regarding her like some girl who was too big for her britches, and who was better placed at the back supporting the men. Instead, Dr. Stone treated her like his equal and was a perfect gentleman.

Overall, Veronica had a great time with Dr. Stone, and she came away with many new connections. The evening couldn't have gone better, and her regard for him had grown by the time she was ready to leave the fair.

Veronica had been worried for nothing.

CHAPTER 18

Jude had searched for a glimpse of Veronica as the fair went on. The dividing walls of the conference rooms on this floor had been collapsed to create one large room, making it easy for him to look for her.

He'd almost given up hope when Tyler, who'd been in California for the past month handling some business matters on Jude's behalf, had come to inform him that a Dr. Brooks was waiting for him. His pulse had raced, and he'd felt his heart lighten. What was it about her that triggered such an effect on him?

But who would have thought he'd have so

much fun at the dental fair? Veronica had listened attentively to the vendors, asked questions, and had been great at making new connections. For some reason, Jude couldn't take his eyes off her, and it had required everything in him to stay focused.

As promised, there'd been a Santa Claus at the event. So far, he'd avoided that section of the room—it reminded him too much of his father who had bailed. Jude's mom had been the one to take Caleb there at the beginning of the event before taking him home.

But Veronica had wanted to visit Santa Claus. How could Jude explain to her it was the last place he desired to be, without looking like a fool? So he'd gone along with her.

Jude had been surprised that all the trepidation he'd had about coming to the Santa Claus zone had disappeared with Veronica by his side. He'd been mesmerized by how much Veronica had enjoyed the visit that he'd forgotten his fears. She'd taken multiple pictures with Santa Claus. Jude had even managed to sneak in a shot of Veronica on his phone as well.

Soon he could tell she was tiring and needed

a breather. "Would you like to take a break in my office?" he asked.

A look of relief crossed her face. "Sure," she replied.

Jude led her to his office—which was decorated in teal and burnt orange colors to give it a light airy feel that worked for patients of all ages —and soon she was relaxed on the custom teal leather couch.

"Would you like something to drink?" he asked. "Tea, coffee, soda, or water?"

"Water would be great. Thanks."

Jude slid a panel open on the wall of his office to expose the refrigerator nestled within, grabbed two bottles of water, and handed one to her.

"Thank you," she said as she accepted it.

He then settled into a chair opposite her and watched as she unscrewed the bottle cap and took a swig. Jude had never thought drinking water from the bottle could be so alluring.

Until today.

Even though it wasn't her intention, Veronica made the act so intriguing that Jude couldn't look away. The grateful smile she flashed him once she was done almost shattered him. It was the prettiest thing he'd ever seen and was so bright Jude couldn't help being starstruck for a moment.

"I needed that," she said. "Thank you." Then a look of concern crossed her face. "Are you alright?" she asked.

Jude, get it together, he thought. "I'm fine," he managed to say. He smiled back at her. "I hope you had fun at the event."

The look of worry left her face, and she relaxed. "I did. Thanks for inviting me."

"I know this was supposed to be your idea. I'm sorry."

Veronica shook her head. "Don't worry about it. You did a far better job, and my event ended up more fun than I expected. So it's a win-win."

His mind flashed back to the kiss at the mention of the Christmas party. *Hold your horses*, he told his mind. He couldn't go there now. Jude was enjoying their current camaraderie, and he didn't want anything to change that. Time to switch the subject. "So, tell me a little more about Dr. Brooks," he said.

She chuckled. The sound of her laughter

stirred his insides. "Me? What do you want to know?"

Jude gave her a lazy smile as he unscrewed his bottle of water. "Anything." He took a gulp.

Veronica dropped the bottle she was holding on the coffee table in front of her and leaned back. "Hmmm. Let me see. I was born in Dexington and grew up here. College and dental school at Harvard. Pediatric dentistry residency at Penn." Those were impressive credentials. "What about you?" she asked.

Jude crossed his long legs. "I was born in Dexington and spent my childhood here."

"Really? Whereabouts?"

"Fernbury."

"Cool. Fernbury has always had a hip vibe to it."

Well, hip wasn't the word Jude would have used to describe the area, but he appreciated her tactfulness. "High school in California. College, dental school, and oral and maxillofacial surgery residency at UCSF."

"Nice! UCSF is a great school." She cocked her head. "So what brought you back to Dexington?"

"My mom wanted to return home, and I

needed a change of pace and a better environment to raise Caleb. So we made the move." Of course, he didn't mention the stalker situation or the girl—now woman—he'd been trying to find since he'd returned to Dexington.

"He's cute."

"You mean Caleb?" Veronica nodded. "He's the light of my life."

"What about his mom?" she asked.

He rarely talked about Caleb's background, but somehow Jude felt comfortable sharing it with her. "I adopted him many years ago after I met him for the first time at a volunteer dental clinic I had organized for kids from disadvantaged homes. Caleb's parents had abandoned him as a baby—he'd been born with a cleft lip and palate—and he was in foster care, but you couldn't tell from how cheerful he was."

"Oh, it's hard to tell he had a malformation from looking at him."

"Thank you. I had the best doctors I could find work on him, though his wasn't as bad as some of the other cases I've seen. We bonded that day, and I decided to adopt him. It was the best decision of my life."

"That was a wonderful thing to do. I would

never have guessed you weren't biologically related from the way you two interact."

Jude smiled as memories of a growing Caleb flashed through his mind. "He's the son of my heart. I'm lucky to have him in my life."

The discussion moved to dental practice in general, and Jude couldn't remember when last he'd had so much fun chatting with anyone.

After a while, Veronica looked at her watch. "Oh! I had no idea it was this late. I need to get going," she said. "Say hello to Caleb. And King as well."

Jude chuckled. "Thanks for saying his name with a straight face."

"I wondered at the name at first. But I figured you had the right to call your dog any name you like."

"He's not mine."

"Really?"

"He's Tyler's. I was just pet-sitting him while Tyler was in California."

"He's a cutie."

"Yes, he is. Do you like dogs?"

Veronica crossed her arms over her chest. "I love them and have always wanted one. But the thought of cleaning up after their mess has always deterred me from making the move."

"That's because you haven't fallen in love with any yet. Wait until that happens, and you'll find the mess becomes nothing."

"Have you?"

"Have I what?"

"Fallen in love with one."

"Yes. And he's Tyler's dog."

Veronica laughed. "How convenient."

Jude grinned. "You can't blame me. The heart wants what it wants." And right now, his heart was desiring something else besides King as his eyes observed the wonderful woman in front of him. But this was not the time to be dwelling on that.

He straightened. "So how about I drop you off?"

"No, thank you," she said with a smile. "It'll only take me a few minutes to walk back to my office."

"It's a little chilly outside. It won't be a bother." Jude had enjoyed their time together so far and wanted to spend more time with her.

"But shouldn't you be back at the fair?"

Jude dismissed her concern. "Tyler will

handle everything just fine in my absence. It's not a big deal."

"Okay. Then I'll take you up on the offer. Thank you."

"You're welcome." He got up. "I'm ready whenever you are."

CHAPTER 19

*V*eronica followed Dr. Stone to his private parking spot behind his office, where a midnight-blue Mercedes Benz G-Class stood under an awning extending from the back of the building.

Nice. She'd learned so much about cars when she'd been shopping for one to buy, and the G-class was one of the ones that had caught her eye. But Veronica had been a long-time Lexus fan, so she'd bought a Lexus IS-250 instead. The awning would come really handy if and when the snow season started. Snow wasn't always guaranteed in Dexington—Veronica had learned that important lesson as a child, when she'd realized she couldn't build a snowman in the backyard like she'd seen other kids do on TV.

Dr. Stone opened the passenger door for her. "Can I help you in?" he said.

"No, thank you," Veronica replied, though she appreciated the offer. "I'll do it myself." Fortunately, she was wearing slacks, which made it easy for her to get in without any wardrobe mishap.

Dr. Stone shut the door after her before going round to the driver's side. Soon, they were out on the street and headed to her office. The sun was already setting in the sky, casting shadows everywhere Veronica looked. Good thing she hadn't walked back alone.

Veronica showed him the way, and before she knew it, they'd arrived close to the front of her office building. The street was as empty as she'd expected, considering that it was after office hours, and most of the other businesses on her street had already closed for the day. More Christmas lights had been hung up on the buildings, and the street now looked like something out of a story book.

Veronica turned to him. "Here's fine. Thank you so much for the ride."

Dr. Stone smiled at her. "You're welcome."

She got out to the sidewalk and then noticed Dr. Stone had hopped out too. "I'll wait until you get in," he said.

"Thanks again." Veronica looped her handbag over her shoulder. She'd enjoyed the evening with Dr. Stone and wished it could continue, but it was time for her to head home after picking up her car and making sure the office had been shut down for the night. She couldn't imagine anything spoiling her mood after the great time she'd had with him.

Veronica strode down the sidewalk and soon reached the bottom steps that led up to the entrance of her building.

She froze, and her eyes widened.

Then she screamed.

CHAPTER 20

Jude rushed to where she stood. His eyes followed her gaze only to see someone had written the following words in red, as if with dripping blood, on one of the glass double doors that led into the building: "Dr. Brooks, you're a slut. You will pay." A crude painting of a skull with a broken X over it completed the picture. The other door had been shattered.

His blood froze. Jude was only too familiar with the image. It was one that had given him nightmares, a symbol that the cops had traced to his stalker, Marilyn Martin, who'd been an art teacher at a local private academy in San Francisco. The cops had done their best to track her down after she'd vandalized his property, but she'd disappeared into the wind.

So this was where she'd resurfaced. The woman was the main reason he'd agreed to leave California. Jude's blood began to boil. Now she'd taken it too far by trying to hurt Veronica.

He wrapped his arms around Veronica and turned her face away from the horror and onto his shoulder. "It's going to be alright," he said. Jude felt her sink against him in relief.

His jaw tightened. This time around, Jude was going to make sure the woman got caught no matter what. Luckily, he had put a contingency plan in place in case she showed up again in his life.

Jude kept Veronica close to him with one arm, pulled out his phone with his other hand, and speed-dialed Tyler.

"Hey, what's going on, doc?" Tyler said teasingly. It was obvious he was still at the fair based on the noise in the background.

"We have a problem," Jude said curtly. "Code Red." It was the "go" signal for his contingency plan.

"I'm on it," Tyler said in a now serious tone.

Jude ended the call, dropped his phone back in his pocket, and wrapped the arm around Veronica. Tyler would call the cops.

Nothing was going to happen to Veronica, not on his watch.

Not if Jude had anything to say about it.

The cops arrived five minutes later, and after examining the scene, taking pictures, and questioning Jude and Veronica, they'd left. Jude had discovered that Veronica had felt she'd been stalked on two separate occasions, one of which had been this evening.

Did it mean Marilyn Martin had been onto Veronica for a while? How had Jude not noticed today at the fair? His stalker radar was usually very good, and his office security already had a photo of Marilyn, which meant she might have been in disguise. He made a note to update his team about it.

The air was chilly, so Jude had pulled out a spare blanket he kept in the trunk of his car, and Veronica now had it around her shoulders. Tyler had also arrived with hot coffee for both of them and quietly informed Jude that the security team he'd contracted for a time like this was already working on tracking Marilyn Martin down. Fortunately, Dexington had more security cameras on its streets than most of their neighboring cities, so the team expected they'd be able to nab her soon. The team's lead had promised to call Jude and the police once they found her.

Jude had also called his contractor, and someone was already fixing both glass doors with the approval of the building's owner. Jude had even informed Veronica's business partner, Dr. Fuller, of what had happened—Veronica had given Jude the number when he'd asked. Veronica had also checked the offices with the police by her side and confirmed nothing was missing. Jude wasn't surprised—it'd been the same way when Marilyn Martin had vandalized his property in the past.

Now he turned to Veronica. "Would you like me to take you home?" Even though Veronica appeared to be back to her calm self, Jude could tell she was still rattled by what had happened.

"Thanks for the offer, but I have to take my car home," she replied.

"What if I drove your car for you?" he offered.

"But what about yours?"

"Tyler will take care of it." He wanted to make sure she got home okay. Jude didn't know where this strong feeling of protectiveness came from, but this was not the time to examine his feelings.

"Okay." She grabbed her things from his car where she'd placed them after the walkthrough with the cops. Jude handed the car key over to Tyler and then followed Veronica to where she'd parked her car. He helped her with the passenger door and her seat belt and then slid into the driver's seat. Soon they were on their way.

"Where do you live?" Jude asked. He knew she lived in a neighborhood close to his because of the run-in with King, but not her exact place.

Veronica told him the address, but otherwise said nothing else on their way there.

They arrived at a quiet street, and Jude was glad to see it was well-lit—he wouldn't put it past Marilyn to circle back to Veronica's home. But Jude was certain, since he'd triggered the contingency plan, that the security firm had assigned a team to follow him here. They would stay behind to watch over the place once he was gone.

"Thank you," was all Veronica said before she exited the car with her things. Jude could tell she was still out of it. It was like she'd withdrawn into herself. He wanted to wrap his arms around her and promise he'd keep her safe, but he had no place in her life to be able to do so.

Instead Jude got out, locked the car, handed the car keys to her, and then watched as she climbed the front steps of her building, opened the door, and then went in. Jude waited a few minutes until the lights came on in her apartment. Then he called a car service to pick him up.

The car arrived a few minutes later, but just as he was about to enter its back door, he heard a noise behind him. Jude turned to see Veronica bounding down the stairs, now dressed in casual jeans, T-shirt, and a short winter jacket. She held an overnight bag in one hand.

"Wait!" she called out. Jude watched her until she reached him. "I'm sorry, but could you take me elsewhere? I'm not sure I want to sleep alone at home tonight."

He understood. It was normal to want to be around people you trust after something like this. "Sure," he said.

Jude turned to the car service, apologized for the inconvenience and gave him a twenty. The hired car drove away.

Then he turned back to Veronica. "Where would you like to go?"

CHAPTER 21

*V*eronica had always enjoyed hanging out in her apartment, which she'd decorated to suit her tastes. But she couldn't sleep here tonight. She needed the company of friends or family, and the orphanage offered both. She could stay with Martha or Elise tonight. "I'll show you the way, Dr. Stone," she said to him. He'd just put on his seatbelt.

"It's Jude," he said. "Dr. Stone sounds a bit too formal."

True. Especially now that she knew him a little better than before. "Then you have to call me Veronica," she replied.

"Works for me."

Jude started her car after Veronica had given him the directions to their destination. Sure, she could have managed to get there on her own, but she had to admit Dr. Stone's presence had been calming for her throughout this ordeal. He'd taken care of everything back at her office without trying to force his help on her, and for that she was grateful.

Her mind went back to the crude writing on the glass door, and she stifled a shiver. Who was the perp? Was it the same person who'd followed her the evening of the Christmas party, and who might have also appeared at the fair this evening? Why? Veronica wasn't sure what to think.

She stayed quiet throughout the drive and was relieved Jude didn't try to engage her in small talk. It was as if he could anticipate what she needed, and it felt good to have him by her side. She'd asked him, half-expecting him to say no, but he'd agreed immediately.

Veronica studied Jude's profile and liked what she saw: dark hair that curled at the base of his neck, graceful dark brows that framed his warm brown eyes, a strong jaw and high cheekbones that perfectly accentuated his features, and those perfect lips that seemed made for kissing. He must have felt Veronica looking at him, because he glanced at her.

Veronica quickly pretended she was asleep. When she peeked at him a few seconds later, he'd faced the road again. But the corners of his lips had turned up in a smile.

Her face warmed, and she quickly shut her eyes. *Shoot!* He must have caught her in the act. Now she had to keep her eyes closed to maintain the ruse.

Veronica didn't know when she fell asleep, and by the time she opened her eyes, the car had slowed to a stop.

They had arrived at the orphanage.

"Thank you so much," she said, stifling a yawn as she sat up.

"You're welcome," Jude replied.

"How do you plan to get home?"

"I'll just call a car service."

But Veronica couldn't have him waiting out here in the cold. The car services were slow to arrive in this area. So she did something she'd never done before, a gesture that could easily backfire and end early whatever it was that was going on between them. "Would you like to come in and wait?" she said.

"Would that be okay?"

Veronica gave Jude a small smile. "Absolutely."

CHAPTER 22

Jude stepped over the threshold and entered the orphanage—he'd seen the small sign on the way in. What was Veronica doing here? Maybe she was a volunteer. But did that mean she could show up at this time of the day? He guessed he'd find out soon.

Suddenly, he noticed the multiple pairs of eyes staring back at him. Kids ranging from three years to teens were standing around the largest Christmas tree he'd ever seen. It was obvious they'd been decorating it before he'd interrupted.

Veronica turned to him. "Dr. Stone, welcome

to St. Andrews Orphanage. Meet my family. Kids, meet my friend, Dr. Stone."

Family. What was she talking about? She must have noticed the confusion on his face, because she said: "I was raised here. This is my family."

Oh! So that was what she meant. Jude wouldn't have guessed in a million years that she grew up in an orphanage. But then he recalled the little girl he'd met years ago who'd been happier than him even with only a guardian. He truly wished he could meet her again. Jude had thought about her every now and then and had even hired help when he'd finally been able to afford it, to try and track her down. But to no avail. It was like she'd disappeared off the surface of the earth, though he had to admit he didn't have much to go on to begin with. Jude hadn't even known her name.

Yet he wished he could find her and thank her for what she'd done. Maybe even get to know her better. She'd met him at his worst, and yet she'd accepted him. Jude also wanted to make sure she was okay, that she'd landed on her feet the way he had. She could very well be married by now, in which case he'd find a way to repay her for her kindness. So as far as Jude was concerned, it was great meeting, yet again, someone who'd done well for herself, despite circumstances she had no control over.

He smiled broadly. "It's nice to meet you all. That's one of the largest Christmas trees I've ever seen!"

Everyone's faces relaxed, and they began talking all at once. Little hands pulled him toward the tree, and soon enough, Jude found himself lifting the young ones to help them hang the ornaments at the top of the tree. Sometimes he hung them himself. It was so much fun, much more than he would have imagined. And the anxiety and phobia he usually felt around Christmas-related activities were absent. What was it about Veronica that helped him let go of his hang-ups about Christmas?

Veronica appeared by his side as if she'd heard her name. "I'm sorry they're keeping you," she said. "I know it's late, and you'd rather be home."

"It's fine," Jude said. "I'm having so much fun." And he meant it.

"Would you like something to drink?"

"Maybe water."

She smiled at him. "Coming right up."

CHAPTER 23

*V*eronica entered the kitchen and pulled a bottle of water from the refrigerator. She'd expected Jude to make his excuses and leave after hearing she'd grown up in the orphanage. Instead, he'd rolled up his sleeves and helped the children decorate the tree. This was a side of him she hadn't expected, but she was loving it.

Elise was already putting plates of cookies and mugs of hot chocolate on trays for everyone. "Could you help me take these to the dining table?" she asked.

"Sure." Veronica added the bottle of water to one of the trays and carried it into the dining area. Elise came behind her with the rest.

"He's a keeper," Elise said with a glance at Jude after placing the trays on the table. The man in question was swinging one of the younger boys into the air.

"Why do you say that?" Veronica asked.

"He's so relaxed with the kids. He even learned about your background without passing out."

Veronica chuckled. "As if that's possible."

Elise put her hands on her hips. "What do you mean? Don't you remember Simone's ex? He passed out right at the front door and then took off when he came to. He ended up breaking up with her the same day via text." Simone had been a few years older than Veronica, and a lovely person. What had happened to her had broken her heart—she'd only dated again after a few years had passed.

Wait! Hadn't it been almost the same for Veronica with the two guys she'd dated? Even her first boyfriend had used her background as an excuse, instead of revealing the real reason he'd broken up with her. Why hadn't she realized this before? *Well, good riddance,* she thought. It wasn't her fault she'd grown up in an orphanage, and she would not apologize for it. She'd done pretty well for herself in spite of it.

She glanced at Jude. Veronica's eyes searched for any forms of discomfort in his body language, but he looked totally relaxed and at ease. He was, for sure, a much better person than she'd originally thought. When he lifted little Mike into the air, an image flashed through Veronica's mind of him doing the same with their kid, who happened to resemble Caleb.

Hey! Get a grip, girl. She wasn't even in a relationship with Jude. Yet … wait, was she already hoping for one with him? *Remember the jinx, Veronica, remember,* she thought to herself. Even though her exes had been douchebags, that didn't mean the Christmas jinx wasn't real. Maybe her best bet was to wait until after the Christmas season to get into a relationship with him. Yes, that was probably the plan that made the most sense, right? Well, that was assuming he wanted one with her.

Veronica picked up the bottle of water and brought it to Jude.

He placed little Mike back on his feet and accepted it. "Thank you," he said and then took a gulp.

"Kids, it's time for cookies and hot chocolate!" Elise called out.

The kids rushed past Veronica and Jude at the speed of lightning to reach the snacks.

Veronica chuckled. She'd been the same way too as a kid.

By now, the children had finished decorating the Christmas tree, and Veronica stood beside Jude to admire it. Christmas lights twinkled like stars from around the tree. Balls of gold, green, and red hung from its branches like heavy fruit ripe for eating. Other ornaments from previous years also draped the trees, and Veronica remembered the memories associated with some of them.

"It looks great," Jude said.

"Yes, it does." Veronica was hyperaware of his closeness, and his sandalwood scent with its hint of fresh citrus reached out to her. She could easily get addicted to this smell if she wasn't careful.

"I have to go," he said quietly.

"I understand. You've stayed even longer than I expected. Do you need me to drop you off?"

He gave her a small smile. "I called the car

service earlier, and he should be here soon." His phone buzzed in his pants pocket, and he pulled it out and checked the screen. "He's here now."

Jude turned in the direction of the dining area and called out, "I have to go, kids. It was nice meeting you all."

"Thanks for your help," Johnny managed to say even with his mouth full.

"Are you coming tomorrow?" Little Mike asked.

"Yes, yes. Please come," the other kids echoed.

"Is anything happening tomorrow?" Jude asked Veronica.

"We have a cupcake decorating contest," she replied. "The cupcakes will be baked by the lovely Elise," Veronica motioned to Elise, who gave a small wave, "and we'll be divided into teams to decorate them. The team that wins gets to decide where the cupcakes will be donated. You can bring Caleb if you like. I'm sure he'll enjoy it."

"Aunt Vee, who's Caleb?" Little Mike asked.

"Dr. Stone's son. He's cute like you."

"Oh, he should totally come," Little Mike said. Some of the kids echoed their assent.

"Would you like me to come?" Jude asked Veronica quietly.

Goodness gracious. Didn't this man have any idea what his low voice did to her insides? Even if she'd wanted to say no, now she had no choice but to respond in the affirmative. "Yes," she managed to say as she tried to hide how flustered she was at his words.

He gave her a warm smile in return.

Veronica's heart skipped a beat, and she cleared her throat as she looked away. What was with her behaving like a teenager who'd just met her crush for the first time? *Pull yourself together, woman.*

"I'll be here," Jude said in a soft voice.

Veronica's heart did a backflip.

"Hey buddy, do you want to come with me to a cupcake decorating contest today?" They were in Jude's living room putting together one of Caleb's favorite jigsaw puzzles. The space was open and airy with large windows that brought in the morning sunlight but also managed to keep out the chilly cold.

Caleb's face brightened. "Really?"

Jude's mom, Lola, a petite, slim woman with steel gray hair that fell to her shoulders, looked up from her knitting. "Where is it taking place?" she asked.

"St. Andrews Orphanage," Jude said.

"Hmmm. I've heard about the place, all good

things too. I've been meaning to go there one of these days to volunteer."

"I'm sure they'd welcome your help," Jude responded. His mom had taken up philanthropy as a second career and loved helping other folks as much as she could. Even now, she was probably knitting something for a child or an elderly patient.

"Have you been there before?" she asked.

"I was there yesterday."

"What did you do there?" Caleb said, his jigsaw puzzle all but forgotten.

"I decorated a Christmas tree."

Jude's mom stared at him in shock. Yes, he totally deserved that. After his father had left, Jude hadn't been big on Christmas, and his mom had caught onto it and eventually stopped buying Christmas trees for their home. So this was huge for him.

Jude had been surprised at himself too. He was usually antsy about Christmas in general, but maybe being with Veronica and seeing the kids around the Christmas tree had done a number on him—all he'd wanted to do was join the fun. And it had been much better than he'd expected.

"Aww! Why didn't you take me too?" Caleb said.

"It was sort of spontaneous, buddy. But that's why I'd like you to come with me today. I told the kids about you, and they'd love for you to come."

"Cool! Okay, I'll go with you," Caleb responded. Then he turned to Jude's mom. "Grandma, we need to go get ready."

"Now?" Jude said. He checked his watch. "We have time."

Caleb rolled his eyes. "Dad, you don't get it, do you? I mean, this is the first time they'll be meeting me. I need to be on point."

Jude's mom chuckled. "Okay, I'll come with you."

"Thanks, Grandma." Caleb jumped to his feet and raced out of the room. Jude's mom followed.

Jude just shook his head. As much as he loved Caleb, he could never understand kids these days.

Jude parked his SUV in one of the parking spots in front of the orphanage and got out. He checked the time—they'd arrived early just as he'd planned. The contest was supposed to start at noon, but he'd wanted Caleb to get a chance to meet the kids before it began.

His phone rang. Jude pulled it out from his jacket and looked at the screen. It was his security team. He swiped the answer button. "This is Dr. Stone."

"Dr. Stone, we've found her," Damon, the head of the team, said without preamble.

Jude's shoulders relaxed. Finally. "Where is she now?"

"The cops have her. San Francisco has spoken to them, and they're taking over the case. Arrangements have been made to transport her safely over there tonight."

"Thank you."

"It's our pleasure, Dr. Stone. We're just glad to finally have her. We'll keep our eyes on the case and let you know if anything changes."

"That would be great," Jude said. "Thanks again. Merry Christmas."

"Merry Christmas to you too, Dr. Stone," Damon said. Jude ended the call.

"Dad, who was that?" Caleb asked from the back seat.

"It's nothing to worry about. Shall we?" He opened the door and hopped out. Caleb did the same.

Jude locked his car and then headed toward the orphanage's front steps with Caleb in tow. The boy had ended up dressed in a bomber jacket over his T-shirt and jeans. A pair of high-top boots completed the ensemble. Jude had to admit he looked good.

The front door opened, and the young lad called Johnny stood before him. He was about Caleb's age and was dressed in a long black winter jacket that extended beyond the knees of his jeans. "Hello, Dr. Stone. Come on in," he said. He glanced curiously at Caleb. "Hello."

"Nice to see you again, Johnny," Jude said as he stepped into the orphanage. "This is my son, Caleb." Jude could see the boys were sizing each other up.

"You look cool," Johnny finally said to Caleb.

"Thanks," Caleb responded.

"You want to play catch in the backyard?" Johnny asked.

"I don't have my baseball glove with me."

"I have a spare one."

"Sure." Caleb turned to Jude for permission.

"You can go," Jude said. "Just be careful."

"He'll be fine, Dr. Stone," Johnny said. "I promise."

Jude watched them take off in the direction of what he guessed was the way to the back-yard. He shook his head. Kids. Pretending to be all grown up, when all they needed to do was remain kids and enjoy their childhood while it lasted.

Now Jude needed to find Veronica. He looked around and spotted her hurrying over from the direction of the kitchen, wearing a long-sleeved woolen dress with cowboy boots. Her vibrant dark hair was pulled into a ponytail.

"You made it," she said, coming to a halt.

"You look beautiful," Jude said.

A hint of blush warmed her cheeks. "Thank you. You don't look too shabby yourself. What about Caleb?"

"He went off with Johnny to play catch."

"Johnny fancies himself a baseball player. He's great at it too."

"Good for him. So can I talk to you for a second?"

Veronica gave him a worried look. "Is everything alright?"

"The person who vandalized your office has been caught. There were warrants for her arrest in San Francisco, so they've taken over the case, and she's being flown there. Long story short, she's no longer a problem."

Veronica's shoulders relaxed. "Did she say why she did it?"

"She—"

"Hello, Dr. Stone." It was Elise. Jude hadn't even known when she'd walked over.

"Good to see you again, Elise," Jude said. Maybe he'd tell Veronica about the identity of the stalker some other time.

She turned to Veronica. "I believe Martha wants to see you," Elise said.

"Do you know why?" Veronica asked.

"Hmm... I might have mentioned Dr. Stone just arrived. See you, bye!" She left like a whirlwind.

Veronica chuckled as she watched Elise leave. Then she turned to Jude. "I was already planning to do so before Elise beat me to it," Veronica said. "Why don't I introduce you to the director?" She led Jude through the house until they reached a large door, which she knocked on.

"Come in," Jude heard faintly from the other side of the door.

Jude followed Veronica into the office. A round matronly woman with lovely white hair cut into a bob looked up at him from behind an oak desk. She removed the pair of owlish glasses that had been perched on her nose, rose to her feet, and extended her hand to Jude. "Welcome to St Andrews Orphanage," she said with a broad smile. "I'm Martha Stockbridge."

Now why did the name Martha ring a bell? Jude racked his brain as to where he'd heard the name, but nothing came to mind. Maybe it would come to him later. "Jude Stone. A pleasure to meet you, ma'am," he said.

Her grip was firm. This was someone who knew what she was about. Jude had a feeling he was going to like Martha very much.

"Jude is an oral and maxillofacial surgeon with a new dental clinic close to mine," Veronica said.

"That's great," Martha said. "Sit." Jude took one of the visitors' chairs, and Veronica claimed the other. "So how are you enjoying Dexington?"

"It's a lovely place," Jude said. "I grew up here."

"Really?"

A knock sounded on the door, and Elise poked her head in. "Sorry to interrupt."

"It's okay," Martha said. "What is it?"

"It's Pastor Stevens. He's been trying to reach you and says it's important."

Martha checked her phone. "Oh. I didn't know I had it on silent mode."

"He says it has something to do with the carol service tonight."

"Okay, I'll call him right back. Thanks." Elise shut the door behind her.

"Don't worry. We'll leave you to it," Veronica said. She rose to her feet, and Jude did the same.

"I'm so sorry," Martha said. "Dr. Stone, it was nice meeting you. I hope we get a chance to catch up soon. Will you be attending tonight's carol service?"

"The one on Seventh Street?"

"That's the one."

"Yes, my family and I had already planned to

be there. My mom had heard how wonderful the service is each year."

"Great. I'll see you there," Martha said.

"Have a good day, ma'am."

"You too."

Jude held the door open for Veronica and then shut it behind himself. "She seems nice," he said to Veronica.

Veronica's face lit up. "She's wonderful. The mom I never had. I'm always grateful to God I've had her in my life."

Martha must have been a big influence on Veronica for her to speak that way. But the name tickled something at the back of his mind. Where had he heard it before? Since he couldn't remember no matter how much he tried, Jude focused on the here and now. "So, where to next?" he asked.

"Why don't we head over to the kitchen?" Veronica said. "The contest should be starting soon."

They made their way there only to see all the kids had gathered outside its entrance.

"What's going on? Veronica asked.

"Elise said she'd call us in shortly," one of the kids responded.

Elise appeared at that moment with a chef's hat on her head. "Welcome, everyone, to this year's cupcake contest. I'm your host, Elise, and I'll be assisted in the judging by Martha."

Everyone clapped, and then it died down.

"This year, we'll be having two groups: one for the girls, and one for the boys," Elise continued. "The girls will be given pink T-shirts with pink scarves, while the guys will receive blue T-shirts with blue scarves."

Caleb and Johnny appeared beside Elise, each carrying a stack of T-shirt packs.

"Caleb and Johnny, could you please hand out the T-shirts?" Elise said. "Everyone, please pick the one with your name on it."

It took a few minutes, but soon everyone had their packs except for Veronica and Jude.

"Dr. Brooks will be the team lead for the girl's group, and Dr. Stone will be the team lead for the boy's group," Elise said. She handed them their respective packs. The T-shirts were in a much larger size than had been distributed to the children.

"We'll give everyone a few minutes to put on their T-shirts," Elise said. "Once you have yours on, please come in and stand behind your table." Jude noticed two tables had been set up on opposite sides within the large kitchen.

He helped the little guys with their T-shirts and scarves, and soon everyone was lined up behind their respective tables. Trays of cupcakes rested on the linen-covered tables as well as piping bags, piping tips, and an assortment of sprinkles, sweets, and cookies of various shapes and sizes.

"I know you've all had a chance to practice on cupcakes throughout the week—well, except for Dr. Brooks, Dr. Stone, and Caleb," Elise said. Caleb raised his hand. "What is it, Caleb?"

"I've decorated cupcakes with my grandma before."

"Awesome." Elise addressed everyone again. "You'll have one hour to decorate the fifty cupcakes in front of you. Each team should choose a theme for their cupcakes. Points will be given for creativity and presentability. No cupcakes should be destroyed in the execution of this contest—points will be deducted if any are damaged. Do you have any questions?" Everyone shook their heads. "Okay. Time starts now!"

Jude had never participated in a contest like

this, but he was going to make sure his team won.

"Dr. Stone?"

Jude looked up to see Veronica smiling at him from the other table. "Yes?"

"You're going down!" She mimed how far down she expected him to go.

Jude laughed. "It's on."

He turned back to his team and gestured for them to huddle together. "So any decorating ideas for the cupcakes?"

"We could go with different colors," one of the kids chimed in.

"That won't work," Johnny said. "The girls will beat us if we do."

"Any other ideas?" Jude asked as he looked from one face to the other. Then Caleb raised his hand. "What is it, Caleb?"

"What if we made a football field with a football on it?"

"That's a great idea," Jude said. "We can use those green sprinkles over there to create the field on top of each cupcake. Then using these chocolate-covered almonds," Jude pointed to the bowl in question, "as the ball, we can place it over the green field and then use cream piping to draw lines on each almond to make it look like an actual football."

"We have the cream piping here," the kid with the round glasses called Little Mike said as he pointed to the bag.

"Yeah, yeah, that's a great idea," the boys echoed.

"But won't the almond just fall off?" another little kid asked.

"So we'll put some frosting on the cupcake before we add the green sprinkles," Johnny said. "By the time we press in the almond on the sprinkles, the frosting should bind every layer on the cupcakes together."

"That should work," Jude said. "So we need someone to put the first layer of frosting on the cupcake, another to sprinkle the green sprin-kles." The boys laughed at the homonym. "Another to put the almonds on the cupcake, and someone to draw lines on the almonds. Who wants to do what?"

Soon the children had split up duties with two kids per role. Jude had them arrange them-selves in an assembly line. He stayed at the end to inspect each cupcake before they were placed on the tray. "Great. Now why don't we start with one cupcake to make sure we get it right?"

Jude watched the kids decorate the first cupcake, and he had to admit the end product looked really good. "Great work, guys," he said. "Now let's do the same for the remaining forty-nine cupcakes."

Soon the kids were hard at work. Jude looked over at Veronica's table and saw they'd made significant progress. But he wasn't worried. His team would catch up soon.

When he checked the time again, they had fifteen minutes left. By now, almost all the cupcakes had received the frosting, the green sprinkles, and the chocolate-covered almonds. The hold-up was with the kids adding lines to the almonds.

Jude pulled in one of the boys handling the frosting, and together the boys and Jude made quick work of the delayed task. By the time Jude added the last line on the final cupcake, there was only a minute left, which he then spent rechecking all the cupcakes and making sure they looked presentable.

Then the alarm went off. "Time!" Elise called

out. "Drop everything in your hands, and step away from your table." Everyone did so.

Jude looked over at Veronica's table, and his jaw dropped. They had created Christmas cupcakes: wreaths, Christmas trees, snowmen, and Christmas lights on the cupcakes, all of which were stunning. How had they managed to design all these in one hour? It was clear they'd beaten the guys and left them in the dust.

Martha came in then and declared the girls the winners. Everyone clapped for them as they squealed at the news and gave each other high-fives. Their team chose to donate the cupcakes to the homeless shelter that some of the older kids volunteered at. Fortunately, Elise had been busy as well and had decorated cupcakes for the kids in both themes, so everyone had a chance to taste them.

Jude picked up one and took a bite. *So good,* he thought as the decadent flavors exploded in his mouth. He finished it quickly and couldn't help grabbing another.

"So what did you think?" Veronica asked, a victorious smile on her face.

"This is really good." He knew that wasn't what she was asking. "Okay, okay, you ladies did a fantastic job with the decorating. But how did you accomplish all that in an hour?"

Veronica grinned. She leaned forward and whispered in his ear. "Did I mention I'm a decorating wizard? Cakes, rooms, name it. It's my hobby." Her breath caressed his skin, and her soft gardenia scent wrapped around him like a warm embrace. Jude fought the urge to pull her into his arms.

But two could play that game. "Really?" Jude said in his most teasing voice. "Maybe I need to find something for you to decorate?" he whispered back.

He saw Veronica swallow quickly, and Jude hid a smile. Then he frowned. What was wrong with him? He was actually flirting with her. But Veronica didn't seem to mind, and it looked like she didn't like to lose either.

"Maybe you should," she teased back in that lyrical voice that turned him inside out. Then Veronica straightened, the corners of her lips curved into a victor's smile. What could he possibly say to that?

"Hello, Dr. Brooks!" Veronica turned in the direction of the voice as Caleb raced to where they stood.

"Hello, Caleb." She extended her hand, which Caleb shook like a proper gentleman. "How are you liking it here so far?"

"Cool," Caleb said. "It's so much fun."

"Did you make any new friends?"

Caleb nodded. "Hmmm. I met Johnny. He's okay."

Jude hid his smile. His son was growing up faster than he'd expected.

"I Just wanted to say hello," Caleb said. He turned to Jude. "Everyone is about to watch a movie. You're coming, right?"

"Yes, we'll be there, buddy," Jude said. He ruffled Caleb's hair.

Caleb jerked out of his reach. "Hey! Not cool, Dad." Then he hurried over to the living room where the kids were already settling on whatever seating area they could find. The floor was not spared.

"We should find seats too," Veronica said.

They ended up sharing an empty loveseat. It had been a while since Jude had watched *Home Alone*, but it was still as funny as ever. When the movie had started, they'd both tried to give each other as much space as possible. But now? Jude had his arm over the back of the loveseat, and

Veronica had settled into him, her head against his chest. And Jude didn't want to change a thing. He wouldn't have minded sitting with her like this for a couple more hours, but like everything else, all good things come to an end.

Once the movie credits rolled, Elise announced that it was nap time for the kids before the evening carol service. Jude saw this as his cue to leave as well.

He rose to his feet, and Veronica did the same. "It's time for us to leave," he said.

"Thanks for coming over," Veronica replied. "I hope you had a great time."

Jude smiled at her. "We did. Thanks for inviting us."

"Let me walk you to your car."

Jude called for Caleb, and together they headed outside. The sun was hidden behind large tufts of clouds, and the temperature had dropped. Jude slid his hands into his pockets, and Caleb did the same.

"So are you taking time off during the holidays?" Veronica asked once they'd reached his SUV.

"Yes. The office is closed until the New Year," Jude replied.

"Same here."

"But I might pop in for a few hours or so at a time to get some administrative work done."

"Still, make sure you get enough rest," Veronica said.

"Yes, ma'am."

Veronica laughed. "Alright. I'll see you tonight."

"Okay. Take care."

"Caleb, see you later." Veronica waved at him.

Caleb waved back. "Bye."

Jude could see Veronica standing there in his rearview mirror as he drove to the gates. He watched her until she disappeared from view when he turned into the main road.

He suddenly missed her. It was as if he couldn't get enough of her—something that was strange to him yet exciting at the same time.

Now more than ever, Jude looked forward to the carol service.

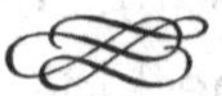

CHAPTER 25

*V*eronica slid into the church pew that belonged to the Dexington family. More than anything, she was glad she could relax and enjoy tonight since the perp had been caught. Even though she would have liked to know why the woman did it, Veronica was just happy to put it all behind her.

"Hey, girlfriend!" Sarah said with a bright smile, her Californian-blonde hair in a ponytail.

Veronica reached for Sarah's son, Blake, who'd been sitting in his mom's lap. He began to suck his two middle fingers as she bounced him on her lap. "He's getting so big."

Sarah beamed a proud mama smile. "I know."

Veronica looked around. "What about Phillip?"

"He's finishing up a meeting and should be here shortly," Sarah said. She glanced at the stage. "I'm so looking forward to the kids singing tonight." The kids from the orphanage had held the first Christmas carol service a few years ago, and now the yearly concert was well-attended by the town.

"I know. And Hannah is joining them too." Geoffrey and Anna had adopted Hannah from the orphanage, but she liked to join the other kids whenever she could. Her performance at the carol service was a crowd favorite.

"What about you?" Sarah asked. She handed Blake his *Sophie the Giraffe* teether, which he promptly chomped down on. "I heard you have a special planned for today."

"Hmm mmm. You know it's been a while, but I'm singing a duet with Clint." Clint had grown up with Veronica at the orphanage.

Sarah furrowed her brow. "Clint? Isn't he the one that works at that consulting firm?"

"Yep."

"Aaah, the one with the angelic voice. I remember you guys used to sing together at the orphanage a lot." Sarah and Veronica had been tight friends since middle school and all through high school, so the orphanage had practically been her second home. "I thought he had stage fright."

"He says he's outgrown it."

"Then I'll look forward to it."

It seemed the program was about to begin. "I have to go," Veronica said. "I'll see you later, alright?" She handed Blake—who by now had drool all over *Sophie*—back to Sarah and rose to leave.

Sarah put a hand on her arm. "Hold on. Is he coming tonight?"

Veronica sat back down. "Who?"

Sarah looked at her like she'd grown two horns. "You know who I mean. The handsome doctor."

"How did you know he was handsome?"

"One, I think I have a good idea of my friend's taste in men."

Well, Sarah had a fair point. The men Veronica liked had to be handsome in *her* eyes. The whole "beauty is in the eye of the beholder" thing. "Two?"

"I looked him up." At Veronica's raised

eyebrow: "Hey, I had to see what the man my friend is falling for looks like."

"I'm not falling for him!" Veronica blurted out as her face warmed. She noticed the people around them had stopped their conversations and were now staring at her. She ran a hand through her hair. This was so embarrassing.

"Shh, lower your voice," Sarah whispered. "Anyway, is he coming?"

"He might," Veronica muttered.

"That's great. I hope I get a chance to meet him. I'm excited for you."

"I can't even reason with you. I'm off." Veronica rose and moved down the aisle.

Sarah chuckled. "Break a leg," she called out.

Veronica gave her a wave above her head as she hurried toward the backstage.

But she had to agree with Sarah on one point.

Veronica was looking forward to seeing Jude too.

Jude arrived at the church with Caleb and Lola in tow. The church was already packed full, and most of the pews were filled. Then he saw someone waving him over from the middle section. It was Elise, dressed in a cream sweater and jeans with her hair in a ponytail.

Jude strode down the aisle until he reached her pew. Johnny was already seated there and seemed excited to see Caleb.

"Hello, Dr. Stone," Elise said.

"Good to see you again, Elise. This is my mother." He gestured to his mom beside him.

Elise gave her a warm smile. "Hello, Mrs. Stone."

His mom was gracious as always. "Please, call me Lola," she said, returning the smile.

"We need to find seats before the program starts," Jude said.

"We have spaces for you here," Elise said. "Veronica asked me to reserve them for you."

Ah, he loved a woman who thought ahead. It was kind of Veronica to do this for him. He had to thank her. "Where is she?" he asked.

"She's backstage with the other kids," Elise said.

"But why is Johnny here? Shouldn't he be with them?"

"I can't carry a tune to save my life, Dr. Stone," Johnny said solemnly.

Caleb chuckled from beside Jude. "Thankfully, I got my singing genes from my dad. He's especially good with 'The First Noel.' It's his favorite." He nudged Johnny. "But I thought you were perfect, Mr. Johnny, if I recall a certain conversation earlier today."

Johnny gave a dramatic sigh. "That's my one fatal flaw, unfortunately." Everyone chuckled.

"I need to get going," Elise said as she stepped out from the pew. "Please go ahead and take your seats. I'll see you guys after the show." She turned to Jude's mom. "It was nice meeting you, Mrs. Stone, I mean, Lola."

"It was great meeting you too," Jude's mom said.

Elise walked away. Jude motioned for Caleb and then his mom to enter the pew, and then he sat at the end. Everyone settled in and waited for the service to begin.

The pastor came on stage and led the church in an opening prayer. And then the concert began.

Jude was enthralled by the voices of the children. It was like heaven opened and the angels began to sing. Then the church choir sang some Christmas songs, which the congregation joined in on, some of which Jude remembered his mom singing from when he was a kid, before his father left. He looked at his mom. Her eyes were filled with tears, and he knew right away that she was recalling the same memories. In that moment, Jude felt terrible for taking Christmas away from her. For not hiding how much he'd hated it, which had made her stop celebrating it all together. For some reason, he'd kept "The

First Noel" close, but every other Christmas-related song or activity had disappeared.

He reached for her hand. "I'm sorry, Mom," he said.

She nodded and patted his hand like she understood what he'd meant. Jude vowed he'd make it up to her from now on. Christmas would be an all-out celebration in his family if he had anything to say about it, anxiety or not.

The church choir ended, and then the children were back on stage. A little girl he didn't know kept everyone in stitches with her antics. She forgot her lines but was quick to improvise, the end result throwing everyone off track. Then the children began a musical play about the birth of Jesus. The whole church hushed in silence as everyone watched them act out the sacred story. Jude was especially moved as he recalled the true meaning of Christmas.

This was what he'd missed the whole time he'd let the abandonment by his father color his lenses about all things Christmas. But no more. Even if it literally killed him to accept Christmas back in his life, Jude would do better, no matter what it took.

Someone tapped him on the shoulder.

Jude turned to see Elise, her face a mask of concern.

"We have a problem," she said.

CHAPTER 27

*V*eronica paced the backstage. "I can't believe this."

"I'm sorry, Veronica," Clint said as he ran a hand through his red hair. "I thought I'd overcome this fear of the stage. I've been doing well at client presentations for some time now, so I didn't think this would still be a problem. I don't know what it is about this stage that gets to me each time."

This couldn't be the end. Maybe they could turn this around. "Take a deep breath," Veronica said. "That's it. In. Out. A few more times. In. Out. How do you feel now?"

"I feel better," Clint said. Then his face

turned green. "Oh shoot. I think I'm going to puke. I'm not sure I can do this."

"Take deep breaths. In. Out." The last thing Veronica needed was vomit splatter all over the backstage.

She rubbed the back of her neck. What was she going to do now? The play on stage was going to finish in a few minutes, and she and Clint were supposed to be the next act. *God help me*, she prayed.

Then the backstage door opened, and Elise stepped in, followed by Jude.

Veronica's eyes widened. What was he doing here?

"He's here to help," Elise said in answer to her unspoken question. "He'll sing the duet with you."

"Thanks, man," Clint said to Jude, relief written all over his face. Turning to Veronica: "I'm so sorry," he said. Then he hurried out through the backstage door.

Veronica blinked a few times. "Hold on. What? Elise, I know you mean well, but this isn't funny. Besides, what if he doesn't know the song? We haven't even practiced together!" Veronica ran a hand through her hair. This was driving her bonkers. She liked Jude, but this was nuts.

"Veronica, look at me," Jude said and waited until she'd turned her eyes to him. "Everything is going to be alright. I know the lyrics to 'The First Noel,' and I'm pretty good at singing duets. Why don't we do a quick trial run, okay?"

Veronica glanced at the stage. The children's play would be over soon. This was not the time to be quibbling. This was her only choice since she didn't really want to be a solo act. "Okay, let's try it," she said.

Veronica took a deep breath and then walked out on stage to a smattering of applause and stood before the mic stand. Jude appeared beside her.

"Good evening, everyone. My name is Veronica Brooks, and I'm here with Jude Stone." Another round of applause. "We'll be singing 'The First Noel' tonight. Please sit back and enjoy." She turned her head and cued the pianist to begin. This was it. There was no going back. It was make it or break it time.

She took another deep breath and then began to sing.

What happened next was almost like an out-of-body experience. Her voice started off soft, reaching out and setting the stage, searching for the hearts that would open up like blossoms to the music. Then Jude took over, his voice smooth, quiet at the beginning yet powerful. A hush fell over the crowd as they listened, enthralled by his every note.

By the time they hit the chorus together, their voices rose and swelled as one, matching each other fiercely, and crashing into the souls of the listeners. Veronica felt each lyric come alive in her heart, tearing off and blowing away the stress and regrets that had lingered, assuring her that everything was going to be alright because of the birth of He who had brought great light into the world. Then they hit the last note, and the sound reverberated and filled the space, proclaiming its last message before ending abruptly.

The room was silent for a few moments, and just when Veronica wondered if it had only been her imagination that they'd been caught up in the song, the room erupted in a standing ovation.

"Bravo! Wonderful!" filled the room as the crowd rose to its feet and gave them thunderous applause. *We did it! We actually did it!* she told herself as her face split into a smile so wide her cheeks hurt. Veronica felt Jude grab her hand. They took a bow and then left the stage.

Veronica pulled him along beyond the back-stage door and into the closest changing room. Then she turned and hugged him tightly. "That was so amazing!" she said. "Thank you." Even though they'd done a quick run through before getting on stage, she hadn't known the depth of his beautiful voice. This was a side of him she'd never imagined.

Jude hugged her back. "Yes, that was pretty awesome," he said close to her ear. The sound snaked its way into her insides. That was when Veronica realized what she'd done. She'd created this private moment!

Her cheeks warmed. What had she been thinking? She made to release him, but Jude pulled her closer, his touch sending sparks through her skin. The butterflies in her stomach began to flutter. His eyes searched hers, and Veronica knew Jude wanted to kiss her.

And in that moment, she wanted him to.

Her eyes must have shown what she was feeling, because he bent his head and kissed her.

It was the lightest of touches on her lips, yet it sent zaps of electricity straight to her core. He tasted so sweet and soft, and Veronica couldn't help wanting more.

She drew his head closer, and then Jude took over. He kissed her hard, stealing her breath, devouring her lips like he couldn't get enough of her. A little gasp caught in her throat. She hadn't expected this side of him, but she loved it too. And then he kissed her softly again, like she was delicate, treasured, and would always be safe with him. Veronica melted inside.

Then he ended the kiss and rested his forehead against hers. His hand caressed the side of her face, sending spirals of pleasure through her. Veronica closed her eyes and leaned into it. She didn't want the moment to end.

"Veronica?" Jude said softly.

"Hmm?" Veronica opened her eyes to see his searching hers.

"Would you go out with me?"

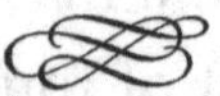

CHAPTER 28

Jude hadn't expected Veronica to hug him, but, in that moment, he'd gained clarity on what he had to do.

It was inevitable.

From the day he'd met her, it seemed everything had happened to bring him to this point. He adored this wonderful woman in front of him, and as much as he shied away from relationships, he knew one thing for sure.

He wanted one with her.

Some might say it was the endorphins pumping through his veins from the duet they'd just sang together that were talking, but Jude knew better. Even though he'd wondered on a few occasions if the girl he'd been searching for was the one for him, Veronica was the beautiful soul right here in front of him, the woman he'd gotten to know, and the one that was slowly wiggling her way into his heart, which he didn't seem to mind.

Veronica's eyes widened at the words he'd spoken. "What?"

She'd heard him the first time, but he'd tell her again if it was what it took. "I'd like you to go out with me and be my girlfriend, Veronica."

Veronica stilled and seemed at a loss for words. Her eyes searched his, and he wondered what she was looking for. But he hoped she saw the sincerity of his heart.

"Yes, I'll go out with you." Jude let out the breath he hadn't known he was holding. "But on one condition."

Now what could that be? "What is it?"

"As long as you watch the fireworks display with me on Christmas Day."

Jude already had plans with his family, but he would make it work no matter what, even though it was only two days away. "What time is it taking place?" he asked. "We usually spend Christmas morning together as a family and then have an early Christmas dinner. The rest of the day is more relaxed. Wait! Now we have to plan together, right?"

Veronica chuckled. "Hold your horses, honey." She noticed Jude's surprised look. "It's just a figure of speech."

Jude leaned forward. "I don't mind you calling me honey," he teased as he tucked her hair behind her right ear. Then he straightened.

It was now Veronica's turn to be flustered. Jude hid his smile as she cleared her throat. "The fireworks display is in the evening after Christmas dinner, and I promised the kids I'll be there," she said. "It's something that my friends, Phillip and Sarah, planned for the kids this year as a Christmas treat. You should meet them. They're wonderful people."

"That works for me," Jude said. Even if it didn't, he would have somehow made it happen. "So, you'll be my girlfriend?"

Veronica hesitated. Then he saw the faint blush on her cheeks. "Yes," she said softly.

Jude had no idea what had made her waver, but he promised himself he'd prove to her that she'd made the right decision.

He drew her close and then bent to give her another kiss.

The door flew open. "I'm sorry," a high-pitched voice said.

Jude and Veronica jumped apart to see an unfamiliar face give them an apologetic look before the door was quickly shut.

Veronica ran her hands down her dress. "I think we should rejoin the service," she said.

"Me too. After you." Jude followed Veronica as they exited the changing room.

But he couldn't help the spring in his steps. Jude couldn't remember when he'd been this happy.

He had a new girlfriend, a woman he enjoyed being with.

How much better could it get?

Christmas Day dawned bright and clear, and as sunny as it could be during winter. Caleb had already barged into Jude's bedroom early this morning, and they'd opened their Christmas presents.

Jude had bought Caleb the steel-string acoustic guitar he'd been wishing for. Caleb had been getting guitar lessons for a couple of years now, after he'd seen Jude strumming one when they'd stopped by a music store—Jude had learned to play after they'd moved to California.

He'd given his mom a temperature-controlled smart mug. Jude's mom loved to have her coffee nearby anytime she was painting, so he'd thought it would be great if she could have it ready by her side at the temperature she always enjoyed. Jude had received a hand-painted portrait of himself, Caleb, and King from his mom. Caleb had gotten him a signed hardback edition from his favorite author and a grey and white winter scarf. His mom or Tyler must have helped him arrange both, but Caleb had emphasized that he'd bought everything with his own pocket money.

Christmas itself didn't seem much different than any other year, but for some reason, everything seemed brighter, more joyous, and hopeful. It was as if this Christmas was the beginning of a new chapter in his life, something he never would have imagined.

Jude knew who had made the difference, and he was looking forward to seeing her today. Since Veronica and Jude parted on concert day, they'd talked a lot on the phone and texted each other. Veronica had needed the next day off to rest, and he'd understood. Everything between them had been a whirlwind, and it was a nice change to take things slow and just enjoy the beginnings of a new relationship. Being in one meant changes for them both, especially since he had a son to consider. For now, they'd agreed to give the relationship a chance to grow before letting Caleb know.

But he had one more thing to take care of before he could really move forward. Jude fingered the pendant he'd worn most weekends from the day he'd met the girl over twenty years ago. It had been a blessing, and thinking of that girl whenever he'd been discouraged had helped him in his darkest moments. He'd carried the torch for her for a long time, even before he'd dated other women, and had held out hope he'd meet her again. Jude would continue to search for her, to thank her for what she'd done in his life.

But it was time to put everything in the past where it belonged.

To make way for a future with Veronica.

Jude opened the top drawer of his night-stand and pulled out a long, dark green box. He removed the necklace and pendant, placed both in the green box, and then slid the box back in the drawer before closing it. Later, he'd take it to the attic where he stored other memories from his past.

Then Jude headed to the living room to relax with Caleb and his mom before the evening fireworks.

"Come on in," Veronica said as she opened the door for Jude.

The temperature had dropped remarkably on his way here, and Jude was glad he'd brought his new scarf along. He'd come alone, as Caleb had fallen fast asleep after the heavy dinner he'd inhaled—it still marveled Jude how Caleb managed to eat so fast.

Jude entered the orphanage, shut the door behind him, and then leaned forward and gave Veronica a kiss on either cheek. She looked breathtaking in a jacket over a grey turtleneck woolen dress and tights, her hair in a cascade over her shoulders, and she smelled deliciously of cinnamon and vanilla. Jude wished he could bottle the scent up. "Merry Christmas, Vee," he said instead. "You look beautiful."

She blushed. "Merry Christmas to you, Jude. Love the attire." Jude had donned a military style winter jacket over a zippered sweater and jeans.

"Thanks," he said. Jude had always looked good in whatever he wore, but he'd paid special attention to his outfit today.

"Come on, let's go out back. Everyone is already there."

She led him through the main area, hallway, and then they stepped out onto the back porch. A low platform had been erected in the center of the back yard, and the kids were lounging on it, all wrapped up in winter wear and ready for the fireworks. They turned to Jude at his entrance and waved. Jude waved back.

"Jude, please meet my friends, Sarah and Phillip. Sarah, Phillip, meet Jude Stone, my boyfriend." Jude's chest puffed up at the word—he was loving Veronica's matter-of-fact style of owning the relationship.

A stunning couple who could have passed for models turned and rose to their feet. The young man, Phillip, who seemed about Jude's age, extended his hand. "Hello, nice to meet you," he said.

Jude accepted the handshake. "A pleasure here too."

"It's great to finally meet you," Sarah said with a twinkle in her eyes. Jude liked her immediately. "I'm sorry we weren't able to connect at the carol service. Why don't you take a seat on the other side of Phillip?" She gestured to the two empty seats beside her husband. "Veronica and I will be back shortly with a drink for you. What would you like?"

"Anything is fine," Jude said.

"Great. We'll be right back." She grabbed Veronica's arm, and they went back into the house. Jude slipped into one of the empty chairs.

"Those two are as thick as thieves," Phillip said. "You know they're going to talk about you, right?"

Jude chuckled. "I guessed as much."

"So how are you finding Dexington?"

"It's good to be back."

"I can't entice you to join Dexington Medical, can I?"

Jude glanced at him. He'd heard about Phillip Dexington and knew he was the sole heir to the Dexington Healthcare empire. Phillip was also an inventor. "But we could always collaborate on something else, right?" Maybe together they could come up with a new dental surgical tool.

"Right. I'm sure there'll be other opportunities." Jude wasn't sure if Phillip was specifically talking about inventions or just meant it in general.

"I heard there'll be fireworks tonight," Jude said.

Phillip nodded. "They should be starting in the next five minutes. It's a new design by an acquaintance of mine. I hope the kids love it," he said with a note of affection in his voice.

"I'm sure they will."

Phillip leaned back in his chair. "I'm guessing you two just started dating."

Jude nodded. It was pretty obvious.

"Does she know? You should tell her if you haven't."

Jude glanced at Phillip curiously. What was he talking about? "What do you mean?" he said.

Phillip stared Jude in the eye. "Does Veronica know how rich you are?"

Jude's eyes widened. Now how did Phillip

know? It wasn't common knowledge in this part of the country, and Jude had planned to keep it that way. He loved his anonymity just fine.

"I try to stay up-to-date on any healthcare industry news across the country," Phillip clarified. "I saw the articles when your company went public. You should tell her sooner rather than later. She hates secrets. You don't want a hopping mad Veronica, I can assure you."

"What do you mean?"

"Just take my word for it. You being loaded as well as having stalker issues are big ones, don't you think?"

Ugh. The guy even knew about the stalker. Jude had guessed Veronica didn't care about the money. But maybe it was his past relationship experience that was making him reticent to tell her before they had a chance to get to know each other better. Besides, he didn't think the stalker issue was a problem anymore—Jude didn't believe there was any need to air his dirty laundry if it was all in the past.

But if Phillip, who had known Veronica far longer than he did, was advocating for it, maybe Jude needed to tell Veronica about his wealth sooner rather than later.

But not today. Today was supposed to be all fun.

He'd enjoy the time with Veronica and then find another opportunity to inform her.

That should work, right?

CHAPTER 29

Sarah pulled Veronica into the kitchen. The space was empty but spotless. Elise must have scrubbed it from top to bottom after the Christmas dinner before retiring to her room for a nap.

"I could have brought a drink for Jude on my own," Veronica protested.

"You didn't tell me he was now your boyfriend," Sarah said. "Have you been hiding secrets from me?"

Veronica rolled her eyes as she leaned against the kitchen counter. "It just happened."

"Just happened, huh?"

'Well, it was after the carol service, and he kissed me—"

"Girl, you move fast!" Sarah chuckled. "You guys have kissed already? How was it?"

"How was what?"

"The kiss!"

Veronica crossed her arms across her chest. "I don't kiss and tell."

"Since when?"

"Since Jude."

They both burst out laughing. After it died down, Sarah said, "You like him, don't you?"

Veronica gave a genuine smile. "I really do."

Sarah cocked an eyebrow. "I thought he was your enemy."

"Haven't you heard: from enemies to lovers?"

Sarah laughed. "You're crazy, you know that?" She pulled Veronica into an embrace. "I'm happy for you."

"Thanks, babe," Veronica said.

Sarah released her. "I'm proud of you for taking the risk, with it being Christmas and all."

Veronica turned serious. "I almost didn't. Then I remembered what you and Sheila had said. If I didn't, I'd always wonder. And I wanted to."

Sarah took Veronica's hand in hers. "You guys will be fine."

"You think so?" Veronica asked quietly, her anxiety about the Christmas jinx rearing its head.

"Yes. But remember that no one is perfect, not even him."

"Okay, I'll keep that in mind."

"Good." Sarah released Veronica's hand.

"So how is little Blakey?"

Sarah smiled. "He's with his grandparents. They're happy to fuss over him."

"You need the break."

"I do. I love the kid, but sometimes I just need some 'me' time."

"I totally agree." Veronica tapped her fingers on the counter. "Jude has a son, Caleb," she said.

"Really?" Sarah crossed her arms over her chest. "How do you feel about that?"

"I'm fine with it. I'm used to having kids in my life. Besides, he's adorable."

"What about his mom?"

"She's not in the picture." It wasn't Veronica's place to talk about Caleb's background.

"Okay. But does Caleb know you guys are dating?"

"Not yet. We want to take things slow."

"That is, if he doesn't already know?"

"But how would he?"

"I'm sure he can guess his father likes you."

'Well, that may be true. Anyway, Jude will tell him when he thinks it's right."

"Okay." Sarah studied Veronica's face. "I'm glad to see you happy. He's good for you."

Yes, he was. The past few days since they'd started dating had been some of the best days of her life. Jude was so down-to-earth yet funny, and she'd enjoyed talking with him. Even if the Christmas jinx was still real and they eventually broke up, she'd have these beautiful memories to hold onto.

"Veronica?" She saw Johnny's head poking into the kitchen. "The fireworks are about to start."

"Thanks," Veronica said.

"You're welcome." Johnny's head disappeared.

"We need to head back," Veronica said. "I'm sure the guys are missing us by now."

∾

The fireworks display was fantastic. Veronica sat beside Jude with her hand in his as the fiery sparks exploded into miniature particles of light. Each colorful streak multiplied into brilliant lines that burned with impatience to tell their stories of Christmas characters, before disappearing in the darkness of the sky. The startled gasps from the kids filled the air as they oohed and aahed with excitement and then guessed what was visible in the sky before it disappeared.

But Veronica was more fascinated with Jude's expressions. He startled at the sudden bangs that accompanied each new firework, yet a bright smile filled his face as he watched the kids' excitement.

Then Jude caught her studying him, and his gaze held hers. Everything else faded, and the air between them crackled with electricity.

Veronica's heart beat faster as her face grew warm. But she didn't look away. It was as if they were the only two people in the universe. Like her soul was bare before him and his before her.

"Merry Christmas, Vee," Jude said softly. Just the way he said her nickname was enough to melt everything within her.

Then he pulled out a gold-wrapped gift from inside his jacket and held it out to her. "This is from Caleb," he said.

Her heart beat with excitement. "Really?" She hadn't expected one from him. She accepted the box and opened it. It was a beautiful pink and white scarf that matched the one that Jude had around his neck. Maybe the little guy did know something was going on between them. "This is so pretty," she said. "Please thank him for me."

"I will. Here's one from me." He handed her a red-and-gold-wrapped gift.

"You shouldn't have," she said. She unwrapped it to see a flat blue box. "What is it?"

"Open it, and you'll find out."

Veronica lifted its lid to see a white gold necklace with a miniature star pendant. She loved how simple yet exquisite it was. She looked up at him. "This is beautiful. Thank you."

"You are the star of my life."

Veronica's cheeks warmed. "That's so cheesy!"

Jude grinned. "I know."

"I love it. Thank you." Then Jude handed her an envelope. "What is this?"

"Open it." Veronica opened the flap and pulled out a voucher for an all-expense paid trip to Disney World for the kids. "All they need to do is call the number at the bottom of the card and the whole trip is arranged."

"Jude, this is too much!" She tried to hand it back.

Jude stilled her hand. "Please take it. I'm sure the kids would love it. It would also be a nice break for them. And it's already paid for, so you can't return it."

It really was a thoughtful gift, and some of the kids had never been to Disney World. "On their behalf, thank you." She pulled him into a hug. "Thank you so much."

"My pleasure."

"I have gifts for you too." She released him and retrieved the gift bag she'd left under her chair. "Here you go."

Jude pulled out a wrapped gift from it and then tore off the packaging to see a small wooden box with his name engraved on it. "What is it?" he asked, his interest piqued.

But he didn't wait for her answer and slid it open to see a wooden pen and its miniature version in the box. He pulled out both, and then his eyes widened as he studied the engravings on them. "Are these—"

"Yes, your initials and Caleb's. I thought he might want one like his dad's."

"These are wonderful." He studied them some more. "And the wood looks unique."

"It is. It's one of those rare wood types—a bocote."

"Nice." He looked up from the pens. "How did you manage these?"

"It's a secret." Veronica had called in a favor.

Jude slipped the pens back into their case. "Thank you." He leaned forward and kissed her."

"Ooooh!" the kids chorused as one.

Veronica's face flushed, and she hid it on Jude's chest. She'd totally forgotten the kids were still outside. Even Sarah and Phillip must have heard their conversation. "This is so embarrassing."

"It's nothing new, Veronica," Sarah called out.

Veronica burrowed her face further into Jude, who chuckled as he wrapped her in a hug. Then she heard the kids shuffling into the house. The fireworks must be over.

Then a familiar ringtone split the air. Who could be calling her?

Veronica straightened and then pulled out her phone from her dress pocket and checked the screen. It was an unknown number.

"Who is it?" Jude asked.

"No idea." She swiped the answer button. "Who is this?"

"May I speak with Ms. Veronica Brooks?" an unfamiliar refined voice said.

"This is she."

"Ms. Brooks, my name is Tim Pierce of Pierce & Bateman LLP. My apologies for calling this late and on Christmas Day no less."

"How may I help you, Mr. Pierce?" She'd never heard of him before. Why would he be calling her? Was this some sort of scam?

"Ms. Brooks, I'm reaching out to you on behalf of my client, your father, Thomas Marsh. I'm sorry to let you know that, unfortunately, Thomas Marsh passed away a few hours ago."

Veronica felt the blood drain from her face, and her vision spun.

The phone dropped from her hand and fell on the ground with a clatter.

CHAPTER 30

Veronica's heart pounded as if to burst from her chest.

No, it couldn't be. Father? She had no parents. She'd been abandoned as a baby on the doorsteps of St. Andrews for goodness sake. How did she suddenly have a father? And if it was true, he was dead. She was only finding out she had a father after he was dead? Why now? Why? All kinds of thoughts crowded her mind, and Veronica felt like screaming.

Jude reached for her. "Hey, what's wrong, Vee? Tell me. Please talk to me."

But what could she say? How could she explain what she'd just heard when she couldn't even believe it herself? Was this some sort of cruel joke? If it was, she was going to murder whoever was behind it.

"Vee, please," Jude said.

Veronica's tongue felt heavy, like it was crushed under pounds of lead. But she had to try and tell him something. She had to relieve the pressure she could feel building in her chest. Otherwise, the weight of it could crush her. "He said I had a father." Her voice sounded unrecognizable even to herself. "And he's dead," she managed in a whisper.

Jude stilled at the news, and then he wrapped his arms tighter around her.

Her phone started ringing again. Veronica covered her ears. The sound was hurting her brain, and she just wanted it to go away.

Jude released one arm and picked up the phone from the ground. "Do you want me to answer it?" he asked. Veronica nodded. She just needed the sound to stop.

He swiped the answer button. "This is Jude Stone. Ms. Brooks is in shock right now and can't come to the phone. But she's given me permission to speak on her behalf."

Veronica released the hands over her ears. She could feel the pressure in her chest receding.

She was happy to let Jude take control—all she wanted to do was hide in a hole and stay there. Veronica was grateful he was in her life at a time like this.

He listened to the person on the other end of the line. "Yes, I'm her family," he said. Those words warmed Veronica's heart, and the pressure in her chest reduced further. "Could you tell me what's going on?" He listened some more. "Okay, I'll let her know," he finally said. "But the decision is up to her. Have a good evening." Jude ended the call and then tucked the phone into his jacket. "Are you alright?" His eyes searched hers as he brushed away strands of loose hair from her face.

Veronica could only nod. That was all she was capable of now.

"Would you like me to take you inside?" he asked softly.

She nodded again. She needed to be alone, away from everyone.

Unlike what she'd initially believed, this was turning out to be the worst Christmas she'd ever had.

CHAPTER 31

"What's going on?" Veronica heard Sarah ask Jude as he rose to his feet with her in his arms.

"Could you please make a cup of hot cocoa for Veronica?" he said, moving toward the door.

"Sure," Sarah replied and hurried inside.

"Is she okay?" Phillip asked as he held the door open for Jude.

"She'll be fine. She just received some bad news."

Jude carried Veronica into the living room and sat her gently on the couch. He removed her jacket and his. Then he sat beside her. "Vee, look at me." She forced her eyes to focus on him.

"You'll be okay," he said softly. "Maybe not right now. But you will be okay."

Maybe it was the softness of his words, but Veronica felt a dam crack open within her, and she began to sob. It was like all the feelings that had accumulated in her heart over the years as a result of being abandoned at the orphanage, even ones she didn't know that were buried deep within, chose that moment to pour out in waves from her, like a river that refused to run dry.

Veronica clutched at her chest as she cried. Her heart felt like it was breaking into pieces, into shards that could never be made whole again.

Yet Jude held her through it all. He didn't rush her but just embraced and soothed her, like she was the most precious thing in the world, letting her know through his touch that he was here for her no matter what or how long it took.

When the tears finally dried up, and Veronica felt all hollowed out, Jude pulled out a monogrammed handkerchief and dried away her tears so gently, as if careful not to hurt her. Once he was done, he held her again in his arms and kissed the top of her head. "Would you like to rest now?" he asked. "We can always talk about it whenever you're ready."

Veronica shook her head. Sarah must be worried by now—Veronica couldn't leave her to wonder what had happened without saying something. "I feel better already," she said. "I'd like us to chat about it and also hear what the lawyer said to you."

Jude released her and handed her a mug of cocoa. Veronica hadn't even noticed when Sarah had brought it. "Thank you," she said. She took a sip, then another, and then drank the rest. The warm liquid coursed through her and restored some of her energy, giving her the strength she needed to handle the difficult conversation she was about to have. "Could you also call Sarah and Phillip? I'd like them to be here if that's okay."

"Absolutely. Whatever you want."

Jude looked over her shoulder and motioned to someone. Sarah came over, perched on the couch on the other side of Veronica, and wrapped her in a hug. "You'll be okay, darling," she said. Phillip had also settled into the loveseat opposite her.

"Do you want to tell them yourself?" Jude asked. Veronica nodded.

"What is it?" Sarah asked. She released Veronica from the embrace but held her hand.

Veronica took a deep breath as she thought about where to start. It was easier to go straight to the heart of the matter. "I just found out I had a dad. He passed away a few hours ago."

"What?" Sarah exclaimed. Her eyes narrowed. "How do you know it's not a scam?"

"The call came from a lawyer at Pierce and Bateman," Jude said.

"I've heard of them," Phillip said. "They are a well-known law firm in the city that specializes in family and estate law. What else did he say?"

"Her father left instructions and a letter for her," Jude replied. "He'd like Veronica to come to his office on the twenty-seventh."

Instructions? A letter? Veronica's brain was having a hard time processing the information.

"Can I see the number?" Phillip asked as he pulled out his own phone and searched for something on the screen.

Jude retrieved Veronica's phone from his

pocket, gave it to her to unlock, and then handed it to Phillip.

Phillip compared the number to what was displayed on his screen. "The number that called her is the same office number that's on their website," he said. He handed Veronica's phone back to her.

"What do you think, Veronica?" Sarah said. "Are you going to go?"

Veronica allowed the question to sink in for a moment. Then she looked up at her friends. "I don't wish to. The man who's supposed to be my father didn't acknowledge me while he was alive, so why now? I'm happy with my life, and I don't want anything from him, so I'm not interested in whatever instructions he left behind. But I'd like the letter. If not, I'd always wonder what was in it."

"Are you sure you won't regret it? The instructions, I mean?" Sarah asked softly.

Veronica thought about it again, but her choice remained the same. It was a decision she would not rue. "Positive."

"Then I think you should call the lawyer back and let him know," Sarah said.

Veronica agreed. She redialed the number and waited for it to go through.

"This is Tim Pierce," the same voice she'd heard before said.

"Hi, it's Veronica Brooks."

"Ms. Brooks, thanks for returning my call. I'm sorry the news was such a shock to you. Please accept my condolences."

"Mr. Pierce, thanks for reaching out. Unfortunately, I'm not interested in any instructions Mr. Marsh left behind, but I'd like to receive the letter. Could you possibly send it to my address?"

"Absolutely."

Veronica rattled off the address of the orphanage. There was no way she was giving a stranger her home address, even if he was from a well-known law firm.

"Perfect. You should receive it tomorrow. Again, my condolences. Feel free to reach out if there's anything else you'd like me to do."

"I doubt that'll be the case, but thank you."

"Have a good evening, Ms. Brooks."

"You too." Veronica ended the call. "He'll send me the letter tomorrow," she said to the group.

"It's going to be alright," Sarah said. She rubbed circles on Veronica's back, which seemed to calm her.

"Thank you, guys," Veronica said. She was glad they were here for her.

Sarah smiled. "That's what friends are for."

Veronica felt exhausted right to the core of her bones. "I think I'll turn in for the night," she said. Then to Jude: "Thanks so much for being here."

Jude touched her cheek. "I'm just glad you feel better."

Veronica managed a weak smile. "Sorry for the lousy date."

"It's nothing. I had a good time. Thanks for the Christmas gifts."

"I loved yours too. Would it be okay if I don't see you off?"

Jude patted her hand. "It's fine. Try and rest tonight, okay? Feel free to call me anytime if you need to talk. I'll always be a phone call away."

Veronica nodded. "I will." She turned to Sarah and Phillip. "I'll see you guys later."

She rose to her feet and trudged in the direction of Martha's room. Martha was away for the night, and besides, Veronica needed the warmth of her bed in her absence.

The revelation that she'd had a father who was now dead was without doubt the worst Christmas gift Veronica had ever gotten.

Yet she was curious what news tomorrow's letter would bring.

CHAPTER 32

*V*eronica stared at the large white envelope for a few minutes. She'd told Elise this morning what had happened, so Elise had brought the letter to her as soon as it arrived. Jude had also called to find out how she was doing and offered to be with her when she received the package. But even though she'd appreciated the gesture, Veronica had wanted to be alone. Now the envelope sat on her lap like an ominous message that was certain to change her life.

And maybe that was why she hesitated to open it.

She let out a sigh. Yet she couldn't put it off any longer.

Veronica reached for the letter opener she'd left on the nightstand and sliced the letter open. Then she took a deep breath before emptying its contents. Sheets of folded paper and a smaller brown envelope fell out. She set the brown envelope aside. Veronica would examine it later.

She flipped the papers open and gasped. The words on them were neatly handwritten, but the handwriting appeared similar to hers, though more masculine. Any doubts she'd had about the person who wrote it being related to her disappeared.

Veronica began to read the first page from the top.

Dear Veronica,

If you're reading this letter, it means I'm dead and have finally passed on to meet your mother.

First of all, I want to say I'm sorry. I'm sorry for abandoning you and letting you grow up all alone. I know this letter is a shock to you, but I wanted you to know that your mother loved you very much. You deserve to know that. You remind me a lot of her.

Your mother and I grew up in a poor neighborhood about thirty minutes away from Dexington. We were high school sweethearts and had planned to marry once we graduated. My own parents had died, and your mother, Lilian Anna, grew up with her elderly grandmother who was old and frail. We had no other relatives. To make a better life for us, I enlisted in the army, and we got married before I was deployed abroad. We'd always dreamed that one day we'd travel together around the world.

Then I got news that your mother was pregnant. I was worried for her since she'd always gotten sick come wintertime, and I wondered how she'd fare with winter approaching. But the pregnancy was all she talked about in the letters we exchanged. She was excited about you and was looking forward to meeting you.

Then her grandmother died in the middle of winter, and the shock sent your mother into labor before she was due. I managed to make it back to her side in time, but though she fought so hard, she passed away right after giving birth to you in her already weakened state. She'd lost too much blood during labor.

My world collapsed. I was so devastated by

your mother's death that I could barely function. She'd been everything to me.

I was discharged early from the army, but even so, your mother's death haunted me. I blamed myself continuously for not being there for her and hated myself deeply at the time.

But there you were, needing so much care, and I wasn't able to pull myself from the dark space I was in to give it to you. Fearful that I might end up bringing harm to you from negligence, I brought you to the orphanage. I'd heard about Martha, and how she cared for the kids as if they were her own. I dressed you in the gown your mother had stitched with the name she'd chosen for you—Veronica Brooks—on it and then dropped you off. I watched from afar to make sure Martha herself picked you up, and then I left. You were better off without me.

I left the country and wandered for many years until I met a lady, someone from our country, in Chile. She helped me slowly come back to myself. We eventually got married and returned stateside.

I realized what I'd done and came back to

look for you. I'd been so stupid. I had wronged you and let you down when you needed me most. But when I saw you were so well-adjusted and happy, I was ashamed to come back into your life.

So I watched over you from afar and arranged anonymous donations whenever necessary to support your education. It was great to see you blossom into a happy and fulfilled young woman, the kind of person your mother always dreamed you'd be.

You resemble her so much. I've included two photographs of your mother in a separate envelope, so you'll see what I mean, along with a brooch that has been in her family for years. She loved it very much, and I'm sure she would have wanted you to have it. On the back of one of the photographs, you'll see some information about where she's now buried, in case you wish to stop by and visit her.

Though it's not enough to make up for what I've done, I've left some inheritance for you and the necessary instructions with my lawyer in the event of my death. Should you choose to reject it, which is perfectly under-standable, the money will be added to the donation under your mother's name to maternal-fetal medicine research at Brigham and Women's Hospital. It would please her to help other women not end up like her.

Veronica, you are beautiful and wonderful and deserve the best in the world. I pray you live the best life you can and share it with a good man who adores you.

Once again, I'm sorry I failed you as a father.

Your unworthy father,
Thomas Marsh

Veronica's eyes brimmed with tears. Her mother had loved her and had been excited about meeting her. She'd looked forward to holding Veronica in her arms, clapping for her when she took her first steps, helping her with her first bike ride, and kissing her knee when she fell down and scraped it.

Her mother had hoped to beam wide smiles when Veronica received her high school diploma on stage and would have gotten a cake for her on her college admission. She'd have been the first to take pictures with her when Veronica got her dental degree, been there for Veronica when she introduced the man she loved, helped her choose the right wedding dress, and given her away when she got married. A small part of Veronica may have held out hope for one of these, but now it was clear she would never have any of them.

She wiped away the tears that had managed to spill down her cheeks. Even though Veronica had always believed it, it was good to confirm she hadn't been abandoned because there was something wrong with her. It was all on her father. Of course, the fear that she'd never been good enough for her family had always been there—a little flame she'd tried her best to stamp out over the years. But it was relieving to finally realize that the fear had always been a lie.

Yet Veronica was grateful she'd been raised in this orphanage, a place where she was loved and appreciated. Though the kids were not related, they'd been more of a family to her than she could ever have asked for.

She laid the papers down gently beside her. Then she lifted the smaller brown envelope and upended the contents. Two photographs and a brooch fell out.

Veronica picked up the brooch and examined the silver design of a little bird in flight but with the eye of a small pearl. Simple but exquisite. She could see why her mother had treasured it.

She placed the brooch on the envelope and then picked up the photographs.

Veronica's eyes widened as she stared at an early-twenties version of herself but in an older time period. In the first, her mother was looking up from the cake she'd been decorating and was smiling. In the second, she was wearing a flowery dress and had her hands over an obviously pregnant stomach, the joy evident in her eyes. Veronica traced her finger over the woman's features, her tears threatening to spill again. Then she flipped the back of the picture and saw the words her father had alluded to in the letter.

The place where her mother was buried.

Giving in to the urge and not second guessing herself, Veronica packed everything back into the large envelope and placed them in her bag. She had to visit the place immediately. She wanted to be closer to her mother, this woman who had given everything to make sure Veronica lived. The cemetery in question was only about thirty minutes away if her memory served her right—Veronica had passed the place once on a trip out of town. She could go there and be back in no time.

Veronica sent a quick text to Jude to let him know where she was going, then she changed, grabbed her bag, and left the room.

Veronica hadn't thought to check before coming, but she was glad the cemetery was open today. She'd followed the directions her father had left, and now she stood in front of her mother's grave in a private lot.

Lilian Anna Marsh. Veronica brushed away the few fallen leaves on her headstone. It was obvious from the manicured lawn around it that the place had been well-cared-for over the years. Though she wasn't sure what arrangements her father had made for its care after his death, Veronica decided she'd make sure it remained this way.

She placed the white flowers she'd brought

on the grave and then sat down on the manicured grass and leaned her head against the
headstone. Where would she begin?

She licked her dry lips. "Hello, Mom," she
managed to croak out. This was the first time
she'd used that word, and a tight knot around
her heart unraveled.

Veronica found it easier to breathe. "Hi,
Mom," she said more confidently but softly. "It's
me, Veronica Brooks."

Then Veronica began to tell her everything
she'd always hoped she'd tell her mother if she
ever had one. From the first friend she'd made
and the difficult times she'd had growing up, to
the first boy she'd kissed. She sometimes
chuckled as she spoke and shed tears a few
times too.

Then finally she said: "Mom, I've found
someone. He's a good man, and I'm hoping
everything works out great between us." She
noticed much time had passed. "I have to go
now, but I'll come again soon. Merry Christmas,
Mom."

She let the words hang for a moment in the
still air. Then Veronica rose to her feet and
dusted the back of her pants.

Her chest felt lighter, like a heavy weight had been rolled off.

She took one more look at the grave and then made her way back to where she'd parked.

There was someone else she really wanted to see now.

Veronica pulled out her phone and made a call.

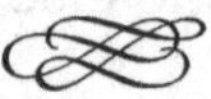

CHAPTER 33

Jude waited in the car in front of her home for Veronica to arrive. He'd raced out of the house as soon as he'd gotten her call—thankfully, Caleb already had a full day of activities planned with Jude's mom. Jude had reached out to Veronica this morning, and even though she'd sounded better, he was still concerned about her. The kind of news she'd received wasn't something he would expect her to get over in a day. He could only imagine how he would have felt if his own father came back. The text from her about visiting the cemetery had only compounded his worries.

Even Caleb had accused him of checking his

phone a million times. His mom had only given him the look but said nothing. All that had been on his mind all day, even on his way here, was making sure she was okay.

He stepped out of his car as soon as he saw Veronica park hers. Then he waited until she crossed the street to where he stood.

Jude pulled her into a hug. "How are you?" he asked. Maybe it was just his imagination but she felt more fragile.

"I'm much better." She nestled further into his arms.

"Come, let's get you out of this cold," he said.

They walked up the front steps arm in arm, and then Veronica pulled the key from her bag and unlocked the door. "Welcome to my humble abode," she said.

Jude stepped over the threshold and then looked around as Veronica locked the door behind him. "Your place is nice," he said. It was very reflective of her personality with its vibrant red, green, and gold furnishings. It held a measure of sophistication and yet exuded warmth and a feeling of home. "Did you hire an interior designer?"

Veronica beamed with pride. "I did it myself. I try to change the colors to match the seasons."

Jude looked at her in surprise. "That's so creative."

"Thank you. Please have a seat."

He settled on the couch—it was very comfy like he'd expected.

"What would you like to drink?" Veronica asked.

"Whatever you have," Jude replied.

"How about sparkling apple cider?"

"That's fine." She soon returned with a bottle of apple cider and two glasses on a tray, which she placed on the coffee table before sitting beside him.

Jude uncorked the bottle, poured the contents into the glasses, and offered her one.

"Thank you," Veronica said as she accepted it.

They enjoyed their drinks in silence, Jude loving the *fizz* effect from the carbonation. Then he placed his empty glass back on the coffee table and turned to Veronica. "How are you really doing?"

"I'm good," Veronica said as she dropped her glass on the table and leaned back.

"Do you want to talk about it?"

"Hmm. A little."

Jude waited for her—this wasn't a topic anyone would enjoy discussing easily.

"My mom loved me," she began. Then she told him what she'd read in the letter, and how she'd wanted to go and visit her mother's grave.

"How did it go?" Jude asked.

"Thankfully, the place was open. I mean I know she's long gone, but it was good to just go there and talk, you know. It was sort of freeing."

"I'm glad you went if it did you good." By now, Jude held one of her hands in his. He loved how their hands fit together.

"I'm glad I did too. So how was your day?"

"I took Caleb swimming."

She lifted her head from the couch. "In this freezing weather?"

"I have a covered pool. It was warm enough for him."

"Your place must be nice."

"It is." Then he told her what street he lived on.

Her eyes widened. "That's close to Sarah's place. That area is expensive. I hope the mortgage isn't crazy."

He shrugged. He probably could have mentioned he was super rich and could afford the place many times over like Phillip had advised, but Jude didn't think this was the time to shock her with yet another piece of news, given what she was going through. He wasn't sure how she would react, and he didn't want to take the risk of finding out. "I can afford the place."

"That's right. I forgot you're a surgeon, not like us poor regular dentists."

Jude just smiled and said nothing. He didn't want to mislead her even if he hadn't revealed the truth.

'So would you like to watch a movie?" Veronica asked.

"Sure. What do you like?"

"I love thrillers and action. Oh, and cowboys."

"Why cowboys?"

"I don't know. They just look sexy in their checkered shirts and jeans. Now pair that with one that can play a guitar. Yummy."

Jude chuckled. "That's quite an image."

"Hey, I like what I like. So what kind of movies do you enjoy?"

"I love romantic comedy and romance," Jude said.

Veronica chuckled. "You're kidding!"

"Why? Men can't like romance?"

"It's usually not the norm," she said with laughter in her voice.

"Well, I like it, and I'm proud of it." He puffed out his chest.

Veronica laughed and hit his chest. "Oh shut it."

Jude caught her hand and held it where it'd landed. "It's nice to hear you laugh," he said.

Veronica looked at him with those warm expressive eyes that got to him every time. "It's nice to have you here with me."

Jude pulled her into an embrace. "I've missed you," he said. He kissed the top of her head.

Veronica snuggled deeper. "I like it here. I'm not sure I want to move."

"So don't." He adjusted so Veronica could rest her head comfortably against his chest.

"So tell me about yourself," Veronica said. "Something most people don't know."

Jude thought for a moment. "I used to have a cleft palate."

Veronica raised her head. "Really? I can't tell."

"It was an incomplete malformation of the soft and hard palate. As you can imagine, I ended up with a lot of surgery, so I spent a long time in and out of the hospital."

"You must have hated it."

Jude nodded. "But the worst part was when my father abandoned my mom and me in the middle of it."

"Yikes. That must have hurt."

"It did. But in that dark moment, I met a new friend and that helped a lot. My mom staying strong beside me did the rest."

"Now I'm curious. I'd like to meet your friend. A he or she?"

"She."

"It would be nice to thank her."

Jude gave Veronica a curious look. "You're not jealous?"

"Why should I be? She was there for you when you needed it most. If you guys were more than friends, then she'd be here instead of me. So when can I meet her?"

Jude couldn't fault her logic. "I don't know

where she is. I never saw her again after that day."

"Did you look for her?"

"As much as I could."

"Maybe she was an angel. Who knows?"

"The thought has crossed my mind."

"I hope you'll meet her again someday."

"I pray so too. So that's my childhood in a nutshell. What about yours?"

"Mine, as you know, was at the orphanage. But it was a good life. The director, Martha, is the best."

Martha. Why did that name ring a bell anytime he heard it? *Think, Jude, think.* He concentrated for a moment, and then it came to him.

Martha was the name the little girl had mentioned! What if Veronica's Martha was the same one? Could it be … ? He grabbed Veronica's left arm and checked. But there was no mole, even though the little girl would have been right around Veronica's age by now. He couldn't help but feel a tinge of disappointment course through him. Maybe he'd wanted Veronica to be her. But could it be another girl at the orphanage? At her age, she would be long gone from the place by now. Nevertheless, it was a lead he couldn't ignore.

"What is it?" Veronica asked.

"Nothing," Jude said. He couldn't ask her about it since he didn't even know the girl's name. There was no need to get her all excited only for it to be a dead end—Jude knew first-hand how disappointing that could be. "Your arm is so smooth," he said instead. And it really was.

"You're funny, you know that?"

Jude gave her a small smile. "Anyway, that's why I decided to study maxillofacial surgery—to help other children like myself. I also run a foundation that sponsors free clinics and surgeries for children with maxillofacial malformations."

Veronica gave him an appreciative look. "Wow, you're a busy man."

"I try. We're blessed to have the support systems we've had, but not everyone has had that. I just try to help."

"True. We've had good lives," Veronica said.

Jude agreed. His life had been wonderful even with the absence of his father, and could only get better with this woman in his arms.

"So shall we watch a movie?" Veronica said.

They spent the rest of the afternoon lounging on the couch as they watched a thriller movie and ended up falling asleep in the middle of it. By the time they woke up, the movie credits were rolling, and the room had darkened a little.

Veronica stretched. "That was a good nap."

Jude had to admit he'd enjoyed it more with Veronica in his arms. "So what do you want to do next?"

"It would be nice if we could do something different that would help me remember this Christmas for something beyond the heavy news I've received. Something that would require minimal effort."

"I can definitely make things fun for you," Jude said and then winked.

Veronica laughed. "Oh please, get your mind out of the gutter."

Jude enjoyed teasing her. "I'm totally harmless. Come here." He only planned to tickle her.

Veronica chuckled. "Are you sure about that?

Jude Junior might not recover from the kick I'll give him."

Jude lifted his hands in mock surrender. There was no way he would chance a kick to his most sensitive area, even if she was just joking.

Veronica laughed. "Checkmate."

Jude chuckled. "Alright. You got me there. How about a fashion show?"

Veronica perked up. "Fashion show? You're joking, right?"

"Leave that to me. I have a favor to call in."

He pulled out his phone and dialed a number.

CHAPTER 34

What happened next was beyond Veronica's imagination. A team of women and men arrived, and Veronica stared in amazement as her open floor plan living space was transformed into a mini fashion runway.

She peered outside her window. The truck that had arrived first was now replaced by a huge bus—the kind she'd heard was favored by musical bands for road trips. It had blocked most of the street, and Veronica prayed her neighbors would not call the cops on her.

"Come sit down," Jude said as he pulled her away from the window and led her to the seats that had been set up for them at the side of the runway.

Then he handed her a catalogue. "This contains all the clothes that will be shown off tonight. Feel free to check off the ones that catch your fancy."

Then the fashion show started. Veronica watched as the models came down the runway dressed in the most beautiful clothes she'd ever seen. And best of all, these were clothes she could totally see herself wearing, unlike what she'd seen on previous fashion shows on TV.

Jude nudged her and pointed to the catalogue, so Veronica began to check off the ones she either found interesting or the ones she thought worked well with her figure. By the time the show was done, she'd selected enough. Veronica clapped for the models as they took their final walk down the runway, off the stage, and out of her house. She assumed they'd gone back into the bus.

Soon an impeccably dressed woman whom Veronica assumed to be in charge approached them. "I'm Céline. I hope you enjoyed the show," she said in a voice with a hint of a French accent.

Veronica smiled at her. "Veronica. Nice to meet you, Céline. Thank you for the wonderful show. The clothes are exquisite, and the ladies did a great job."

Céline beamed with pride. "Did you see any you liked?" Veronica nodded.

"You can give her the catalogue," Jude said. Veronica handed it to her.

Céline looked it over. "Great choices. Give us a minute, and we'll bring the ones in your size." She left the apartment with a man Veronica assumed was her assistant in tow.

Veronica leaned toward Jude. "I'm going to try them on now?"

"Sure," Jude said. "You don't want to?"

"It's fine. I'm just surprised they have my size. How does she even know my size?"

Jude chuckled. "She's an expert. You'll see."

The man returned with an armful of garment bags. "Where would you like me to place these?" he said.

"Down this way." Veronica led him to her guest room. Thankfully it had a full-length mirror.

The man placed the bags on the bed and then exited as Céline entered, closing the door behind her. "I'll help you," she said.

Veronica stepped out of her clothes, and

Céline helped her into the first dress. It was a knee-length silk dress of the softest pink with an intricate ruffle design around the neck and bishop sleeves. It gave Veronica an ethereal look which she loved. Céline handed her a pair of strappy gold heels that were her exact size. A gold teardrop necklace and matching earrings completed the look.

"Oh my, you look stunning," Céline said.

And Veronica believed it. The color brought out the different shades of brown in her eyes. Now what would Jude think?

Veronica stepped out of the room and headed to the living room. Jude was by the window and turned at that moment.

The world seemed to halt. Jude was at a loss for words, and the look of adoration in his eyes almost undid her. "You look beautiful," he finally said.

Veronica's face warmed. "Thank you." Jude smiled. It was as if he could see her blush. "Okay, I'll go try on the others." She hurried off before he could say anything else.

She returned to the guest room and tried out the remaining clothes before choosing the four outfits she loved.

"These are wonderful choices," Céline said.

Veronica gave her a hug. "Thank you so much. I had so much fun."

Céline smiled widely. "It was my pleasure." They stepped out of the guest room.

"We'll take the shoes and accessories as well," Jude said.

"That's too much," Veronica protested.

"Anything for my angel," Jude said. Then he turned to Céline. "Thanks so much, Céline."

"Always a pleasure, Dr. Stone. Feel free to call us any time."

"Will do," Jude replied.

Veronica waved as Céline left with her team. Then she jumped into Jude's arms and gave him a quick kiss, then another. "Thank you!"

"I should probably do this more. I'm loving these kisses."

Veronica rolled her eyes and nudged his arm. "Oh please." Jude chuckled. "But how did you do it?"

"I met Céline after I helped her family in the past, and she became a good friend of mine."

"Does she live in Dexington?"

Jude shook his head. "In New York. But she

just opened a branch of her business here, so she's been in town this past week."

"Thank you. I had so much fun."

"I'm glad you loved it. Now let's get some food into you."

It turned out Jude had ordered some food while she'd been trying on the clothes, and it arrived a few minutes later. They spent the rest of the evening laughing and eating dinner.

Soon it was time for Jude to leave. "It's time I headed home," he said.

"I'll walk you out," Veronica said as she shrugged on her jacket.

"No, you don't have to. It's cold outside." He pulled her into his arms.

"I had a great time," she said.

"Me too." Then he kissed her forehead and her two cheeks, before giving her a soft kiss on her lips, like she was the most delicate jewel in the whole world. "Take care of you, okay?" he said.

She nodded. "Say hi to Caleb and your mom."

"I will." Then he kissed her once more, released her, and then left her apartment.

Veronica stood by the window and watched him leave. She was exhausted but happy.

Jude had brightened her mood and had been the most attentive boyfriend ever. She'd gotten to see again how wonderful he was. It had been amazing, almost unbelievable, how quickly he'd managed to organize the fashion show. But most of all, she treasured the time he'd made for her in his life.

The night had been perfect, and she couldn't imagine anything affecting this new joy she'd found.

Veronica fell asleep with his name on her lips.

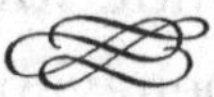

CHAPTER 35

The shrill sound of her phone pulled Veronica from the deep sleep she'd been in. *Ugh.* Yesterday had tired her out, and she'd planned to spend the morning in bed. Who could be calling her this early?

She picked up her phone from her nightstand. "Veronica speaking," she said as she answered the call without looking at the caller ID.

"Dr. Brooks, this is Dr. Fuller."

Sleep fled from Veronica's eyes, and she sat up. Why would Dr. Fuller be calling her? The office was closed until after the New Year. "Good morning, Dr. Fuller. Is everything okay?"

"Unfortunately, I have bad news."

Veronica's heart thudded in her chest. What could it be this time around? "Go on."

"I just got a call from the building owner, Mr. Jones, to inform me that he's put the building up for sale," Dr. Fuller said. "He says he received an offer he couldn't refuse."

"But he never said he was planning to sell the place!"

"I know. He's been receiving offers for a while now, but only became interested after the vandalism incident."

Veronica rubbed her forehead. This couldn't be happening. "So will the new owner take over our lease?"

"That's the problem. The new buyer is looking to renovate the building completely, so they're only willing to give us one month."

"One month? That's ridiculous!"

"He says the buyer is more than ready to compensate us whatever we need to move out and get a new place. Mr. Jones is willing to help us find someplace in the neighborhood that works for us."

Veronica ran her hand over her hair. This was a mess. One month to find a new place, set it up, make sure it passed inspection, and get all the licenses they need while meeting their patient appointments? She didn't see how that was possible. There had to be some tenant rights they could exercise to delay this. "Can we talk to him to change his mind?"

"I doubt he will."

But it was worth checking into just in case. Veronica had nothing to lose. "Could I have his number? I'd like to try."

"Sure. I'll send it to you right away."

A moment later, Veronica heard a ping. She checked to see that a text message with the number had just come in. "Thanks," she said. "So what do you think we should do?"

"I think we may need to close the clinic," Dr Fuller said quietly.

No, she hadn't heard right. "What?"

"I'd been meaning to call you before Mr. Jones reached out. Kelsie just had twins two days ago." Kelsie was Dr. Fuller's only child who lived in Arizona with her family.

"Congratulations," Veronica said. But what did it have to do with the practice?

"Well, now she has four kids to take care of, and it's too much for her, especially with her husband working long hours in the ER. Mary has been wanting us to move closer to them because of the grandkids, and this seems to be the final push. So we've decided to pack up and relocate. The initial plan was to discuss this with you after the New Year and ask if you were interested in buying my share of the practice. I know you may not have the funds for it right now, so I'd planned to draw up an agreement where you'll make payments over time until the transaction is completed. I expected it might take up to three months to complete the transition."

Veronica laid her head against the headboard. This was a lot to take in. "So why shut the clinic now?"

"Well, Mr. Jones has only given us a month. Mary and I have to pack up our home, which means I won't be able to focus on moving the clinic to a new location and setting it up. It's just easier for me to shut it down and refund your share of the practice. Given the demand in the market, the time should be more than enough for the team to find new employment. But I'll make sure they get compensated for the abrupt closure."

Veronica didn't know what else to say. She

couldn't stop Dr. Fuller from helping his only child, and yet she couldn't imagine the clinic shutting down. All the work they'd done before the holidays would be for nothing. And the team was her family. There had to be a way. "I'm more than willing to buy your share of the practice, Dr. Fuller."

"I guessed you might say that, and I'm glad for it. But it would mean you'd have to move the clinic alone."

Veronica squared her shoulders. She could do this if it came down to it, but she would explore her options about the building with her lawyer first. "I'll do it."

"Great. I'll get my lawyer on it, and we can discuss more after the New Year. I'll also make sure there is temporary help to cover my cases until you get a more permanent solution."

"That works for me."

"Sorry for blindsiding you with this, Dr. Brooks."

"It couldn't be helped."

"Have a wonderful New Year. Feel free to reach out if you have any questions."

"I will. Happy New Year to you too." Dr. Fuller ended the call.

Veronica dropped her phone and collapsed back on the bed.

Why couldn't she catch a break? Here was another problem just when she'd thought everything was going to be smooth sailing from now on.

There was no way she could move the clinic out within a month. She had to find a solution, but she had no idea where to begin.

Her doorbell rang.

Veronica looked up. Who could it be? She wasn't expecting anyone.

She threw a robe around herself and padded out of the bedroom. Soon she reached the front door and looked through the peephole.

There was no one there.

Strange. She had to be careful—she was a single woman living alone.

Veronica unlocked the door without removing the door chain and peered through the narrow opening. She found nothing … except a small box at the foot of her door. Had it been the mailman?

She removed the door chain, picked the box up, and carried it inside, making sure to lock her door again.

Veronica placed the box on her kitchen table and examined it. It was addressed to her and had a single mailing label on it. She grabbed one of her knives and opened the package.

There was a stack of pictures inside. It occurred to her that maybe she shouldn't handle them with her bare hands. Thankfully, she'd always kept a box of sterile gloves on hand. Doctors in general tended to do that. So Veronica headed to her medicine cabinet, retrieved a pair of gloves, and then returned to pick up the pictures from the box.

They were numerous pictures of the same woman—a slim attractive-looking blonde—with Jude at various locations. And the last one showed Veronica and Jude kissing at the Christmas party. The following words were written in bloody red over it: "He's mine. You will pay." The image of a skull with a broken X leered at her from the bottom right corner.

Veronica gasped in fright.

The pictures fell from her hands and scattered like confetti all over the floor.

CHAPTER 36

*J*ude reread the email he'd drafted one more time and then clicked *send*.

Done. He stretched his limbs. It was great to be able to come into the office and catch up on administrative work without being interrupted.

The building was empty save for Tyler, who was also working in his office a door away. Today was only meant to be a partial workday— it was the holiday season after all.

His mind went to Veronica. The time he'd spent with her yesterday had been epic. They'd laughed and chatted a lot, and he'd gotten to know more about this enigmatic woman he was drawn to. There was something about her that made him comfortable enough to put down his walls, and he was beginning to realize he wanted more of her in his life—it was as if he couldn't get enough.

Jude adored this lady, who could be both fierce and shy, and he thanked God he'd met her. If anyone had told him that the woman he'd thought was a stalker was now precious to him, he would have laughed the person off the street, no, off the planet. But now, she was all he could think about.

Then the memory of his father flashed through his mind like a warning.

Jude froze. He'd looked up to him, yet the man had left when the going got tough. Everything was great with Jude and Veronica right now, but what if she left when things became hard? No matter how rich he was, he wasn't immune to life's troubles. Jude didn't think she would. Yet how could he be sure? He'd been best buddies with his father, and he'd never thought the man would abandon him.

Jude made a decision. He had to be careful, no matter how much he wanted to open his whole heart to Veronica. It had taken him a while to heal from his father's betrayal—which had also caused his Christmas phobia—and get to this point. So maybe it made more sense to take things slow.

His phone rang. Jude picked it up, and he perked up as soon as he saw the caller ID. Just the person he'd been thinking about. "Hello, Vee," he said cheerily.

"Jude." Her voice sounded weary and tired.

Jude straightened. Had something bad happened? "Is everything okay?" he asked.

"Would you mind coming over to my house?"

"Now?"

"Yes."

"I'll be right there. Are you alright?"

"I'll see you soon," Veronica said.

"Okay. I'll be there shortly." She ended the call.

Jude jumped from his chair and grabbed his jacket. Something was definitely wrong. Whatever it was had to be really bad if Veronica didn't want to talk about it on the phone.

He strode from his office. Another problem was the last thing she needed.

So whatever it was, Jude was going to take care of it.

CHAPTER 37

"Come on in." Veronica stood aside to let Jude in. She'd changed into a pink T-shirt and jeans, and was glad she had, because he looked delectable in a red-blue-white polo over blue jeans.

Down, girl, she told herself. She had a bone to pick with him, and this was not the time to be distracted. Why hadn't Jude told her he knew the stalker? She hoped it was a simple misunderstanding.

"Is everything okay?" he asked.

"This way," she said curtly. She led him to the kitchen and noticed when he spotted the box and the photos all spread out on the counter.

Jude froze. "Where did this come from?" he asked.

Veronica ran a hand over her head. "That's what I want to know. Jude, who's this woman? Is she the one who vandalized my office?" She couldn't help that her voice shook with anger.

He peered closely at the box including the mailing label before straightening. "Why don't we take a seat?" he said.

Veronica allowed him to lead her to the couch, and then he sat across from her. He had good instincts if he'd guessed she didn't feel like having him next to her right now.

"To answer your question, yes, she's the one who vandalized your office," he said. "Her name is Marilyn Martin."

Veronica crossed her arms over her chest. "You know her." It wasn't a question.

He let out a sigh. "Yes, I do. I met her once on a blind date arranged by a friend, but chose not to see her again because of the vibes I got from her."

"What do you mean?"

"I'd had a previous girlfriend who was obsessed with me to the point of stalking. After I broke up with her, I didn't date for a long time.

Then my friend suggested the blind date. I owed him a favor, so I went along with it to appease him. Then it became obvious she knew way more about me than I would have expected for someone who'd just met me. She sort of blipped on my stalking radar.

"I made it clear that nothing could happen between us. But then she started showing up uninvited around my office, my home, and even events that I attended."

That was creepy. "But what about these pictures? It seems like you guys were together everywhere."

He ran a hand through his hair. "Those are photoshopped. I was out with other folks at those events. She swapped them out and replaced them with herself. You can send them to a forensic expert if you want to verify. I eventually had a restraining order out against her, but that didn't stop her. She ended up vandalizing my home, and by the time a warrant was out for her arrest, she'd disappeared. She's one of the reasons why I was glad to leave California behind."

"But then she showed up here. Why didn't

you tell me who she was the night she vandalized my office?"

"At first, I needed to make sure she was the one responsible. Then I tried to tell you right before the cupcake competition, but Elise interrupted our discussion. I should have found another time to inform you, but it totally slipped my mind with everything. I'm so sorry."

Veronica leaned back on the couch. She remembered Elise had cut them off in midconversation. "So where is she now?"

"She's in custody. She was arrested the morning after the incident and then transferred to California where she had a list of pending arrest warrants a mile long. It seemed I wasn't the only one she'd been obsessed with. From what I've been informed, they have a slam dunk case against her and don't expect her to be out for a long time.

"From the time stamp on the mailing label, I believe she sent this box before she was arrested, so I doubt you'll receive another. We can hand this box over to the cops, or if you like, I can have my security team handle it accordingly."

Veronica wanted the box out of her house as

soon as possible. "You can take it with you. I'll be happy if I never see anything like this again."

"It won't happen again."

She wasn't sure if he could promise her that, but she'd take him at his word. "Okay."

"So are we good?" Jude asked. He seemed earnest about it.

Was he thinking she'd end the relationship because of this? Veronica wasn't that shallow. It wasn't his fault he'd been stalked.

She gave him a smile that she hoped reassured him. "Yes, we're good. You're not getting rid of me that easily."

He chuckled as his shoulders relaxed. Then his eyes searched her face. "You look tired," he said.

"It's nothing," Veronica responded quickly. There was no way she was telling him about the news from Dr. Fuller. She could handle this problem herself like she'd always done. Besides, she'd seen from others that money issues tended to kill a relationship quickly.

"Okay."

She wasn't sure if he believed her, but she was glad he didn't probe any further. Now that he'd taken care of this issue, she needed some time alone to figure out what to do about the clinic.

Veronica rose to her feet. "I have some important stuff I've been meaning to take care of."

Jude got up as well. "I'll leave you to it. How about dinner tonight?"

Veronica wasn't sure if she could get through it without spilling her gut about her problem. "I'll take a raincheck. But we can chat later tonight if you like."

"That works." He pulled her into his arms. "Veronica, you're important to me," he said as his mouth brushed her ear. "I won't let anything bad happen to you."

Veronica almost spilled her secret at his words. It would have been nice to have someone else to share the burden with. Still, it wouldn't be fair to Jude to saddle him with it.

So she pulled away and gave him a smile instead. "Now go before I lose my resolve. I really need to work on a few things."

He chuckled. "Okay."

"And don't forget to take *that* box with you."

"Yes, ma'am."

CHAPTER 38

Jude reached the door to Tyler's office and poked his head in. Tyler was typing furiously on his laptop and looked up at the interruption.

"In my office. Now," he said.

Jude didn't wait for his response and headed to his office. Soon Tyler's brisk steps caught up to him just as he entered.

"What's going on?" Tyler said.

"Catch." Jude threw the box, which he'd sealed off in cellophane wrap from Veronica's kitchen, in his direction.

Tyler caught it perfectly. "What is this?"

"Marilyn Martin." Jude didn't need to say more.

He strode to the sink in his office and washed his hands. He wished he could scrub off everything that had to do with that woman.

"When did you get this?" Tyler asked.

"Veronica received it today." Tyler cursed under his breath. Jude dried his hands and walked around his desk to plop in his swivel chair. "Don't worry. She sent it before we caught her."

"Do you think she set any other tricks in motion?"

"Who knows? I doubt it. But we should keep an eye out just in case."

"On it. I'll make sure Damon gets this."

"Thanks."

"So how are things going with the good doc?" Tyler settled himself on the couch in the office.

"What do you mean?"

"You're here instead of being with her."

"She has some stuff to take care of." Though he'd wondered if something else was bugging her from the way she'd looked. "*We*," Jude gestured to Tyler and himself, "also have things to attend to."

"Right. As if that would have stopped you

from dashing to her place if she so much as crooked a finger in your direction. It's clear you have the hots for her."

"Nothing wrong with that imagery."

Tyler chuckled. "Are you still the same Dr. Jude Stone I know? The one that said, if I remember clearly, that he'd never date again, ever?"

"That's the difference the right lady makes. You, my friend, need to find the right woman."

"Please. They're all the same. Well, with some exceptions. Like Ms. Lola."

Jude pointed a finger at Tyler. "My mom is off limits, in case I haven't made myself clear."

Tyler chuckled. "Noted. But don't be shocked if you get a new stepfather in the future. Your mom's too good to be left alone, and she deserves someone wonderful too."

"Can we close that discussion? You, on the other hand, need to try opening up your heart. It'd be good for you."

Tyler made a face. "No thanks. I'll leave all the lovey cheesy stuff to you."

Jude's phone rang, and he pulled it from his jeans pocket. Only a select group of people had the number, but it wasn't a number he recognized. He swiped the answer button. "Hello."

"Good day, Dr. Stone. This is Dr. Fuller."

Wasn't that Veronica's colleague? Jude remembered calling him the night of the incident. "Good morning, Dr. Fuller. To what do I owe the pleasure of this call?"

"I need your help," Dr. Fuller said. He detailed what was going on with the clinic. "Dr. Brooks can handle some of the general cases, but a few require specialist orthodontist care. I'd like to refer those to you until Dr. Brooks finds a replacement," he finished.

"I can take care of those patients for you," Jude said. "I have two orthodontists on my team, and we can make it work."

"Thanks. I assume Dr. Brooks would be more comfortable dealing with you. I've also heard good things about your clinic, so I'm sure the patients would be in good hands."

"Thank you for trusting me with them."

"Great. I'll inform Dr. Brooks of our arrangement, and I'll have her handle it from here."

"Sounds good."

"Have a good day, Dr. Stone, and Merry belated Christmas."

Jude chuckled. "You too, sir." He waited until Dr Fuller ended the call, and then he tucked his phone back in his jeans pocket.

"Who was that?" Tyler asked.

"Dr. Fuller." Jude frowned. "It seems there's something going on with the building owner. He's selling the building. Can you look into it and get back to me ASAP?"

"On it." Tyler jumped to his feet, already at work on his phone, and headed out of the office with the box tucked under one arm.

Jude swiveled his chair from side to side. This was likely what had preoccupied Veronica's mind. He couldn't even imagine how she must be feeling at this moment after getting this news. Jude had no idea how she planned to handle it, but he was going to do everything in his power to help. He remembered when a certain little girl had given him his wings when he'd needed it most. Now was yet another chance to pay it forward to someone else.

He heard footsteps and looked up to see Tyler was back. "How did it go?"

"The man is more or less ready to seal the deal with a certain buyer, but he'll be motivated enough to consider us if we come up with a better offer. I was able to find out what the current bid is."

Jude tapped his fingers on his desk. "Let's offer him twenty percent more and make it an all-cash offer valid only for the next three hours. He'll be wired the funds as soon as he signs the deal."

Tyler grinned. "You want him to accept your offer immediately. What about the inspection contingency?"

"We'll skip it in this case. I'm spending that money for Veronica's peace of mind, and I want to close this deal as fast as possible. Besides, the building is on prime real estate. Even if we pull it down completely and rebuild, we'll still make our money back in no time."

"Okay, I'll get it rolling."

"Thanks. And one more thing, I need you to look into the records at St. Andrews Orphanage to see if the little girl lived there."

"You found something?"

"The director is Martha Stockbridge. I finally remembered Martha was the name the little girl told me."

"The name you couldn't recall," Tyler said.

"Right."

"That should be helpful. I'll send the information to the PI. I'll also let you know once the building deal is done."

"Thank you." Tyler turned and left the office.

Jude placed his hands behind his head as he leaned back in his chair. He'd always been grateful for the chance to have enough wealth to last a lifetime, but he'd never been more glad for it than now, with the chance to help someone he really cared about.

But he wasn't certain if independent Veronica would feel the same way about it.

CHAPTER 39

Veronica gulped down the water and placed the glass in the sink. She'd wash it later. She had to call Mr. Jones now.

She'd finally gotten through to her lawyer in the afternoon, and he'd confirmed she had options that could help delay the move. However, he'd cautioned her it might be better to go with the deal offered by the landlord, if he was willing to compensate them fully for the inconvenience, and if the details of the compensation were clearly stated in writing and notarized. But Veronica also believed she had nothing to lose from attempting to convince the landlord to change his mind.

She checked her watch. She still had some

time before closing hours. Veronica wasn't sure what Mr. Jones' schedule was, but she'd rather not call late in the evening. She picked up her phone and dialed the number Dr. Fuller had given her. It rang twice before someone answered on the other end.

"Jones speaking."

"Good afternoon, Mr. Jones. This is Dr. Brooks from Fuller Dental."

"Ah, the doctor that works with Dr. Fuller."

"Yes."

"So how may I help you, Dr. Brooks?"

"Dr. Fuller has informed me you're selling the building."

"Yes, the building is sold."

Veronica's heart sank. Already? Now all her plans to persuade him to give them more time were moot. One month to move was crazy. What was she going to do now? She had to try something, anything. "Can I meet the new owner?" she asked.

"I can let him know you'd like to meet. But it would be up to him to reach out directly."

It wasn't what Veronica wanted, but it was better than nothing. "Okay. Thanks. I'll be waiting for his call."

"Have a good evening, Dr. Brooks." Mr. Jones ended the call.

Now Veronica only had to wait.

Which, as it seemed, was the most difficult part.

CHAPTER 40

"She wants to meet you."

Jude looked up from the dental journal he'd been reading on his tablet. He'd spent the morning so far catching up on news in the industry. "Who?"

"Dr. Brooks. She wants to meet the new building owner." Tyler left the door open and stepped further into Jude's office. Jude's offer had been accepted within an hour, and he was now the brand new owner of yet another commercial building in Dexington.

"Did she say why?"

"Jones didn't ask."

Jude leaned back in his chair. There was no way he could let that happen. It would destroy his desire to remain anonymous. "You know that's not possible."

Tyler hunched over one of the visitors' chairs in front of Jude's desk. "Don't you think it might be better to come clean?"

"I'm not sure that's a good idea."

"I know you have your reasons, but you can't keep the truth from her forever."

"I doubt the tenants of my other buildings in California know that I'm the owner."

"Fair point. So what should we do? We both can't go. And the real estate team didn't handle this deal."

"I'll do it," a familiar voice said.

Jude looked up to see his lawyer and friend, Louise Parker, stride into the office, dragging her carry-on luggage behind her.

"Louise!" Tyler gave the tall brunette a hug. "When did you get here?" he asked and then released her.

"A few minutes ago."

"Welcome to Dexington," Jude said. "Hope you had a good trip."

Louise gave him a broad smile. "I did. Thanks for sending the car to pick me up."

He smiled back. "It was nothing." Louise

was here on an unrelated business trip, but Jude was taking the opportunity to catch up on some business matters back in California related to the company he'd sold.

Louise settled on the couch. "So the meeting with the tenant. Let me take care of it," she said.

"I'm not sure that's a good idea," Tyler said.

Jude glanced at Tyler. "Why? Louise already handles most of my business dealings anyway."

"Just saying," Tyler said.

Jude gave Tyler a curious look. This was the first time Tyler was being cryptic when opposing an idea. He was usually the more vocal one.

"It's not a big deal," Louise said. "All I'll need is a brief summary."

"And Tyler will give that to you," Jude said. "Thank you so much."

Louise flashed him a warm smile. "You're welcome."

Jude was only too glad he'd dodged the bullet.

It was settled. Now everything should work out just fine.

CHAPTER 41

*V*eronica took a sip of the soda she'd ordered as she waited in the lobby of the May Crown Hotel. Men and women in business attire conversed as they lounged on single high-backed seats spread out across the center of the high-end hotel. Natural light from the midday sun streamed in through the floor-to-ceiling glass walls, but it didn't seem to bother the occupants of the tables lined along the walls. Veronica had only been here once for a conference, and the place remained as busy as she remembered it.

"Dr. Brooks?"

Veronica looked up to see a stylish young

woman in a blue pin-striped pantsuit carrying a slim dark red briefcase. "Yes."

The woman gave her a warm smile and extended her hand. "I'm Louise Parker."

Veronica stood and shook her hand. "Nice to meet you. Please have a seat." The lawyer had called her on behalf of the building owner a few hours ago and requested to meet. Veronica had been happy to oblige. She'd called Dr. Fuller, and he'd given her the go-ahead to make decisions at the meeting as she saw fit.

Ms. Parker slipped into the seat opposite her. "Thanks for meeting me here. I had a business lunch earlier and figured it was just as good a place to meet as any."

"That's fine. Would you like anything?" Veronica asked.

"I'm good. Maybe we should get down to business?"

"Sure."

"So you wanted to meet the new building owner."

It was time to make her case. "Yes. I realize the ownership has changed, but we'd like to keep the current lease as-is."

"Mr. Jones mentioned he'd given you a month's notice."

"But it would pose a significant hardship for us. We need more time to make the transition, though we'd prefer to remain in the building if possible."

A set of blue eyes regarded her. "The owner is fine with keeping the lease as-is," Ms. Parker finally said.

Veronica felt a boulder of worry roll off her shoulders, and she relaxed. "Thank you."

"But on one condition."

She tensed. So it had been too good to be true. "What is it?" she asked.

"We would like to carry out some renovation."

Veronica wasn't sure she understood what Ms. Parker was getting at. "What do you mean?"

"We'll do it in such a way that it doesn't affect the clinic. Most of the work would be done after hours and over the weekend."

Veronica's forehead furrowed. "But is the rent expected to go up as a result?" The practice would have to make some cutbacks if it went up, and it was already running a tight budget as it was.

Ms. Parker waved her concern away. "The rent will remain the same, even after the renovations. The owner is a big supporter of healthcare and its services."

Veronica leaned back and let out an exhale. She'd been worried for nothing. This was even a much better deal than she'd imagined, and she was fine with the renovations. Maybe the practice might even save some money—the owner might end up taking care of some of the upgrades Veronica and her team had penciled in for the next quarter. But then she remembered her lawyer's suggestion. "Can we put this in writing?"

Ms. Parker smiled. "I figured you might say that." She opened up her briefcase and pulled out some papers, which she passed to Veronica. "Here you go."

Veronica accepted the papers and reviewed the two sets of documents. They looked fine to her, and she didn't see any red flags that might have necessitated a review by her lawyer. Besides, the papers clearly stated that the existing lease remained in effect. So she pulled out her pen and signed the documents on behalf of the practice. Ms. Parker signed as well, then handed a copy to Veronica and slipped the second set back into her briefcase.

"Thank you so much," Veronica said.

"You're welcome. Any other questions?" Ms. Parker asked.

"I think we're good for now."

Ms. Parker laughed. "You're interesting, Dr. Brooks." She glanced at her watch. "Unfortunately, I need to be on my way." She stood. Veronica did the same. "Have a wonderful day, Dr. Brooks."

Veronica smiled at her. "You too, Ms. Parker."

She watched as Ms. Parker stepped away and soon left the hotel.

Veronica flopped back on her seat. Now she needed another drink.

Thank goodness it was finally over. Nothing else could go wrong now.

CHAPTER 42

"*H*ow did the meeting go?" Jude asked Louise. They were in his office—Louise sat on the couch, her briefcase beside her.

"It went well," Louise replied as she crossed her legs.

"Thanks for helping out."

"You're welcome. Dr. Brooks is beautiful. I can see why you like her."

Jude glanced at her in surprise. "How did you know?"

Louise shrugged. "But does she know you're not interested in marriage?"

"We're not at that stage yet."

"But you shouldn't lead her on. It's better she knows up front."

"I'll think about it."

"I have to go," Louise said.

"So soon? How about staying for dinner? I'm sure my mom would be glad to see you."

She rose to her feet. "Maybe some other time. I have a business meeting early tomorrow morning in San Francisco I need to make. Please extend my regards to her."

Jude got up. "I will. Let me arrange a car to pick you up."

She gave him a small smile. "All taken care of." Her phone pinged, and she checked the screen. "My ride is here."

"Let me see you off at least."

She shook her head. "Really. There's no need. Besides, I have to stop by Tyler's office on my way out. He'll see me off." She came around and gave him a hug. "It's good to see you happy. Good luck," she said softly.

Jude hugged her back. "Take care of yourself, okay?"

"I will." She released him. "I'll talk to you later." Then she grabbed her briefcase and left his office. Jude watched her shut the door behind her.

He settled back into his chair and leaned

back. Frankly, he hadn't thought about marriage just yet. Sure, the mere suggestion of marriage was usually enough to send him in the opposite direction, and for good reason. But now? The idea of marrying Veronica and having kids with her didn't scare him like before. Instead, the thought excited him.

Interesting.

How could he have changed so much in such a short time? The only difference was Veronica was now in his life. Did it mean she was all he'd been waiting for? Jude needed to think more about this.

But, on the other hand, what if Veronica didn't want the same thing? That possibility didn't sit well with Jude. *Very strange.* But there was no point speculating on it on his own—the only way to find out where she stood on the issue was to ask her directly.

His door swung open, and Tyler strode in. "I just saw Louise," he said. "Did the meeting with Veronica go well?"

"Yes."

"That's surprising."

"What do you mean? And, by the way, what was that cryptic response about her meeting Veronica? That's unlike your loud self."

Tyler cast him a disbelieving look. "Don't tell me you don't know."

Jude straightened. "Know what?"

"That Louise has had a crush on you this whole time."

Tyler had to be joking. "That's not possible."

"Why not? She's single and wonderful."

"She's my lawyer and friend. I've never done anything inappropriate to make her think otherwise."

"Dr. Stone, you can be dense sometimes. And yes, you can dock my pay for saying that. Don't you get it? All our friends in California know. You're the only pigheaded person who doesn't seem to be aware. So how do you think she felt meeting the one person that had conquered your heart?"

Jude rubbed his forehead. "I had no idea."

"Does it change anything?"

"Change what?"

"Does knowing Louise cares for you change how you feel about Veronica?"

"No, Veronica is the only one for me." Jude ran his hand through his hair. "But what do I do about Louise? I never planned to hurt her." He jumped to his feet. "I have to talk to her. I can't pretend that I don't know now that I do."

"You might catch her in front of the building by now. She'd planned to stop by the guest office and pick up her things."

Jude hurried toward the door. "Thanks."

He raced through it and down the hallway. How had he not noticed? Louise had always been dear to him, but firmly in the platonic zone. He considered her more of a sister than anything else.

Soon he saw Louise opening the back door of a grey town car parked in front of the building.

"Stop!" he said as he hurried through the revolving door and out the main entrance.

Louise glanced at him. Her eyes were red-rimmed. "I have to go, Jude," she said in a thick voice and made to enter the car.

He reached for her arm. "Please, Louise. Just give me a few minutes." He couldn't let her leave all upset. She turned to him and buried her face in his shirt.

Jude fidgeted. He'd planned to comfort her, but not like this—the last thing he needed was any more misunderstandings about their friendship. "Louise …" He tried to extricate his shirt from her grip.

"What's going on here?" a voice he recognized demanded.

Jude's heart dropped.

CHAPTER 43

*V*eronica froze, not sure what she was seeing in front of her. There was no way this was real.

She'd guessed Jude was at the office and had wanted to surprise him with the good news about her office building. So imagine her surprise, after crossing the street from where she'd parked her car, to see another woman in Jude's arms right in front of his building. Veronica gasped as she realized who she was. It was the lawyer, Ms. Parker!

How? "What's going on here?" Veronica demanded.

Jude dropped his arms like he'd been burned, and his eyes jerked in her direction like he'd been caught stealing cookies from the cookie jar. From the way he'd held Ms. Parker, it seemed they were very close. Closer than would have been expected in a mere friendship. And how did he even know her? Meeting Ms. Parker twice today couldn't be a mere coincidence. For some reason, she couldn't connect the dots.

"Do you know her?" Veronica asked Jude, her calm voice belying the turmoil of emotions coursing through her. *Please tell me the truth*, she prayed.

But Jude said nothing. It was as if he'd been frozen and rooted on the spot.

"Please tell her the truth," Louise said softly to him.

Veronica's heart sank. The truth about what? Their relationship? "Tell me what, Jude?"

But it seemed Louise couldn't wait for his response. "I'm Jude's business lawyer."

Lawyer? In his embrace like this? Who was she kidding? There had to be something more between them. And she'd called him by his first name.

"Vee, please—"

"It seems more than a business relationship

to me," Veronica said, ignoring Jude's attempt to speak to her.

Louise sighed. "Jude is my good friend as well as my client. He was just consoling me about something, so there's no need to read any meaning into it. I represented him earlier today when I met you."

Friend. Lawyer. Building. The words swirled in Veronica's mind until they coalesced into a single cord. "You mean?" No, it couldn't be. There had to be some sort of explanation

"Don't," Jude whispered.

"I'm sorry, Jude, but she has to know," Louise said. She turned back to Veronica. "Jude is your building owner."

Veronica staggered back. *No!* How was that possible? Dentists were paid well but not *that* well. Real estate in this area was very expensive. "How? How can he afford it?"

"You didn't know?" Louise said with surprise in her voice. "Jude is a billionaire."

Another big secret. It was like a death knell had been rung. *Unbelievable.* Everything had been lies, all lies. Veronica spun to him. "Are you even a dentist?"

"Yes, I am," Jude said. "Vee, please let me explain." He reached for her.

Veronica gave him a look that could have set his whole body on fire. "Let go of me." She wrested her arm away. She'd thought he was different, but he'd broken her heart just like the others. "You lied to me." She couldn't stay and hear anymore. "Don't follow me."

Veronica turned so he couldn't see the tears that had pooled in her eyes.

She hurried in the direction of her car, hopped in, and drove away, not waiting to see if he'd followed.

But tears ran down her cheeks as she navigated her way through the streets, headed in the one direction where she'd always found comfort.

She'd failed yet again in another relationship, though this one felt like her heart had been ripped out of her chest.

It seemed Veronica couldn't escape the Christmas jinx in her life after all.

Jude paced his home office. He'd hailed a passing cab and followed Veronica yesterday until she'd arrived at her destination, which turned out to be the orphanage. Then he'd returned home.

Louise had left for the airport and had called to apologize about how things had turned out. But he didn't blame her—it was all his fault. He should have heeded Phillip's advice. He still kicked himself for having frozen when he'd heard her voice in front of his office. He should have hurried to explain what had happened. Now he wasn't sure if Veronica would ever speak to him again.

He plopped into his custom swivel chair, jumped to his feet, and then collapsed back in it again. He'd called and messaged her several times, but she'd ignored his calls. He knew she needed time to sort through everything, but what if she gave up on him in the process? Jude couldn't afford to lose Veronica. He hadn't understood how much she meant to him.

Until now.

And he'd hurt her—the last thing he'd ever wanted.

What was he going to do?

Jude heard the door creak open, and he glanced toward it.

His mom entered and sat opposite him, looking as stunning as always in a cream blouse paired with white slacks. "What's going on, Jude?" she asked.

He looked down at his hands. "It's nothing," he said.

"I'm not leaving until you tell me what's going on. You've been so frazzled and on edge throughout the day. Even Caleb knows something is wrong."

Jude felt a pang of guilt. He'd been distracted

the whole time he'd been with his son. He ran his hand through his hair.

"It's about Veronica, isn't it?"

Jude's eyes widened. He hadn't had a chance to introduce her to his mom. "How—"

"Caleb told me about her. She sounds like a fine woman. So what's going on?"

Jude told her everything that had happened. When he'd finished, his mom reached forward and smacked him on the arm.

"Ouch! What was that for?" Jude said as he rubbed the reddened spot.

"For being stupid. Even I knew Louise had a thing for you, but I didn't say anything because I didn't believe Louise was the one for you."

"Why do you say that?"

"Louise is a wonderful woman, but you treated her like a sister. You never had that sparkle in your eyes or spring in your steps, which I'd almost given up hope of ever seeing. Until a few days ago. After you met Veronica. That's who Veronica is to you."

Jude hadn't known his demeanor had changed that much.

His mom wasn't finished. "But most of all, Caleb adores her. He's always liked Louise, but not like this. I know I haven't met her, but I've loved what I've heard about her so far. And don't let the failed marriage between your father and me hold you back. Do you love her?"

Jude hadn't thought it was ever possible, but Veronica had broken down the barriers in his heart and made him want to be a better everything both to her and to his family. He couldn't imagine life without her. "Yes, I love her," he said.

"Then fix this."

"But how?" He had no idea what to do.

His mom patted his hand. "I'm sure you can come up with something. Use that high-powered brain of yours." She rose to her feet.

"Thanks for the pep talk."

"You're welcome. Now go." She left his office.

Jude rubbed his forehead. Speaking to his mom about it had removed the heavy load that had weighed him down. But what was he going to do? He had to convince Veronica to give him a chance, and he needed to let her know he was here to stay and wasn't going anywhere.

Then an idea struck him.

Jude jumped to his feet and grabbed his coat and his car keys.

This could either be his worst, most embarrassing mistake or the best idea ever. He would either sink or swim with it.

But first he had to speak with Caleb.

CHAPTER 45

Veronica had her legs up on the couch as she watched a Christmas movie with some of the kids. Elise had coaxed her from the room, where she'd isolated herself, to join them. But she could barely register what was on the screen. All her thoughts were on Jude.

He'd withheld the truth from her. Jude could have easily told her he was the new building owner. Why had he kept it from her? Then he'd also hidden the fact that he was a billionaire. Did he think she was a gold digger? Didn't he trust her? Veronica didn't hate money but just disliked those who used it to tear others down. Jude hadn't seemed that way, so why had he withheld that information from her? Veronica hated secrets, and Jude had delivered double. Now her heart ached from the betrayal.

Yet she missed him.

She'd had no idea he'd become so entrenched in her heart. She'd seen his missed calls and had been tempted each time to call back, but her heart was not ready. She needed more time.

"Veronica, do you want a cookie?" It was Little Mike standing in front of her and holding out a chocolate cookie, while pushing his glasses up his nose with the other hand.

She gave him a small smile. "No, thank you, Mike. I'm not hungry."

Elise gave her a surprised look from beside her. Veronica knew what she must be thinking— Veronica had never turned down a cookie at the orphanage. But ever since she'd left Jude, every-thing had tasted like ash in her mouth.

Then Veronica heard a sound. Who was playing that guitar? It didn't sound like recorded music. "Can you hear anything?" she asked Elise.

"I think it's coming from that window."

By now, the kids had heard it, and they all ran to the window that faced the parking lot.

But Veronica stayed on the couch—she was too tired to move.

"Veronica, I think you need to come and see this," Elise said from where she stood close to the window.

"What is it?"

"Just come and take a look."

Veronica rose and padded over to the window. The kids made way for her until she was close enough to see into the parking lot.

Her mouth dropped open. Jude was dressed in a checkered shirt, jeans, boots, and a cowboy hat and was playing the guitar. She'd told him about cowboys being sexy, but she hadn't imagined he'd play it out in real life!

Veronica didn't know whether to laugh or cry. The song called to her like a moth to a flame, yet her feet stayed rooted on the spot as she remembered how he'd hurt her.

"You should go to him." Veronica turned to see Martha by her shoulder. "He's a good man."

"I thought so too. But he lied to me."

"Why do you think he lied to you?"

Why hadn't he disclosed he'd bought the building? A thought occurred to her. Could it be...? "Maybe he didn't want me to reject his offer."

"Would you have?"

Veronica thought about it for a moment. Her strong sense of pride would have made her reject it. "Yes."

"Would rejecting it have harmed you?"

"Most likely." She would have been running around by now trying to find a new space if the previous buyer had bought the building.

"So he did it for you."

"But he also lied about being a billionaire."

"Maybe he's had people chasing him for his wealth, and he wanted a real relationship. Or do you care about his money?"

"Absolutely not."

"Has he disrespected you in any way because of money?"

"No."

"Has he done anything else to hurt you?"

"No." They'd been pretty good together. And he'd been a great support regarding the news about her parents. He also hadn't run away once he'd found out she grew up in an orphanage. Instead, he'd accepted the family she had.

"Can you imagine life without him?"

Her heart squeezed in pain at the thought of never seeing him again. She shook her head.

Martha nudged Veronica's shoulder. "Then go get your man. You know today is pretty cold, right?"

Veronica didn't have to be told twice. She gave Martha a quick kiss on the cheek. "Thank you." Then she raced to the coat closet, grabbed two jackets, donned one, put on her boots, and rushed outside as quickly as possible until she was standing in front of him.

Jude stopped playing as she approached and adjusted the guitar until it was at his back. "Hello, Vee," he said in that voice she'd missed.

She wrapped the spare jacket around his shoulders. "It's cold. Come inside."

"Not without saying what's on my mind. I'm sorry, Vee. I'm sorry for not telling you how rich I am, and that I'd bought the building. Dr. Fuller called and told me what was happening with the clinic. He wanted my orthodontists to cover his cases until you found a permanent replacement. I bought the place so you wouldn't have to move, but I was afraid you might reject my offer if I told you about it. You mean the world to me, and I just wanted to make things a little better for you. But I should have discussed that directly with you and given you the option to make that decision yourself.

"I should have told you I made a lot of money from selling a dental device company I'd created with my business partner. I've been targeted by gold diggers in the past or judged for my money, so I wanted a relationship where I was seen for who I am and not for what I have. Because Vee, the Jude you've met is the same with or without the money. But I was wrong, and I hope you find it in your heart to forgive me."

He rubbed his forehead. "I also wish you'd cursed me out to my face instead. I was hurt that you shut me out of your life completely without giving me a chance to explain. I think it's always better to talk through things together no matter how difficult it is to do so."

Veronica wrapped her arms around him, and his citrusy sandalwood scent filled her nostrils. "I forgive you, and I'm sorry too. I should have given you a chance to explain. I know you meant well about the building. Thanks for doing that for me."

Jude hugged her back. "I've missed you." Then he shivered. "I forgot my jacket on the way over and had no idea it would be this cold."

Veronica grinned. "What's up with the outfit?"

"Just trying to be your sexy cowboy." He winked.

Veronica laughed. "You're more than perfect, my sexy cowboy." She stood on tiptoe and gave him a kiss on the lips. The kids hollered from the window at that.

Jude chuckled. "These kids."

Veronica grinned. "They're the best. Now, let's get out of this cold before we freeze to death."

Veronica laughed as Elise shared a joke. She couldn't believe Jude was here, sitting by her side on the couch. As if he knew what she was thinking, he flashed her a quick smile and squeezed her hand before returning back to the conversation with the others in the living room. Veronica leaned into him, and he drew her closer to his side.

Then Jude checked the time, got to his feet, and cleared his throat. "I have something to say," he said. The room quietened.

"What are you doing?" Veronica said.

Jude turned to her. "Veronica, you blew into my life like a hurricane." Everyone in the room laughed.

Veronica's cheeks warmed. What was he thinking?

"But now, I can't imagine my life without you," he continued. "You're the most beautiful, wonderful person I've ever met, and you have a heart of gold."

She heard a loud knock on the front door, and Veronica groaned inwardly. Who could be disturbing this beautiful serenade she was receiving?

Johnny raced to the door and opened it. Soon Caleb came into view.

Veronica jumped to her feet. "Caleb, what are you doing here alone at this time? Is everything alright?"

Caleb grinned. "Tyler brought me." Veronica glanced at the entrance to see Tyler leaning against the wall beside it. What was going on?

Caleb coughed, and Veronica's eyes swung

back to him. He pulled out a small black box from his winter jacket and opened it.

Veronica gasped. The most beautiful diamond—set in a band of white gold—stared back at her.

"Dr. Brooks, could you please marry my dad and be my mom forever?"

By now, Jude was on one knee. "Veronica, please marry me and make me the happiest man on earth."

Tears filled Veronica's eyes. This was the last thing she'd expected, yet she couldn't imagine life without them both. Caleb had honored her by asking her to be his mom—a position she'd gladly accept with all her heart. And they'd both proposed to her in front of the people that mattered most to her. Her family. "Yes, Caleb, I'll be honored to be your mom. And Jude, yes, I'll marry you."

She held out her left hand, and Jude lifted the ring from the box and slipped it on her finger. Then he swept her off her feet and gave her a mind-blowing kiss that had her toes curling and her insides melting.

Her family didn't disappoint—they cheered and clapped as loudly as ever.

Veronica only grinned, her heart filled to the brim with joy.

She'd finally come home.

"Are you sure I look okay?" Veronica asked Jude as they sat on the large couch in his living room. She'd insisted they come back immediately and meet Jude's mom. But now that she was here, she couldn't help how nervous she felt.

"You look beautiful," Jude said and winked at her. They'd stopped by her house on their way here, and Veronica had changed into a purple woolen coat dress and put her hair up in a chignon. He took her hand in his. "She already loves you." Veronica had to believe it.

"You look great, Dr. Brooks," Caleb said. "And Grandma is wonderful."

Veronica gave him a warm smile. "Thanks, Caleb."

A gorgeous, middle-aged lady in a dark blue cashmere dress and steel gray glasses that matched her hair entered the room. If this was his mom, Veronica prayed she'd age as beautifully as she had. A wide smile split her face as she approached them.

Jude and Veronica rose to their feet.

"Veronica, please meet my mom," Jude said. "Mom, meet Veronica Brooks, the love of my life."

Jude's mom pulled Veronica into a hug. "It's so great to finally meet you, dear. Please call me Lola or Mom, whichever you prefer."

Mom. She liked the sound of it. "Yes, Mom."

Jude's mom's smile widened. And in that moment, it filled a hole in her heart Veronica never knew existed.

She'd finally found her own family.

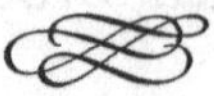

CHAPTER 46

The next day, Veronica laid the flowers she'd brought on the headstone and then straightened. She stepped back and put her hand in Jude's. Caleb stood on her other side.

"Hello, Mom. It's me, Veronica," she started. "I wanted to introduce some pretty special people in my life to you. Mom, please meet Jude Stone, my fiancé and your soon-to-be son-in law, and my son-to-be, Caleb Stone. I thought you might like to meet them."

Veronica told her mom how she'd met Jude, everything that had happened between them, and how Jude had asked her to marry him. Jude then promised to take care of Veronica with all his heart and keep her safe.

"Mom, you don't have to worry about me now," Veronica said. "I'm going to be just fine, and I have my own family who loves me very much." She brushed off a stray leaf that had fallen on the headstone. "I have to go now. Bye, Mom."

Veronica took Caleb's hand in one hand and Jude's in the other. "Let's go," she said.

Her heart was full, and she had everything she could ever need.

They were relaxing in the dining area after spending a wonderful time chatting with Jude's mom. His mom had gone to take a nap, and Jude was preparing snacks in the adjoining kitchen. Veronica was drawing with Caleb at the table.

"What do you think?" she asked him of her drawing of Jude working in the kitchen.

"Dr. Brooks, I love you, but this is awful." Veronica laughed and tickled him. "Hey, stop that," Caleb said, though it was obvious he was loving every second of it.

"It's because I'm not drawing with my

favorite pen," she said.

"Yeah, right."

"Seriously. It makes a difference."

"I think I know the one," Jude said from the kitchen. He was wearing an apron, and Veronica loved how dreamy he looked in it. "I believe I have one in my nightstand." Jude had shown her where his bedroom was yesterday when he'd given her a tour of the house.

"Okay. I'll be right back."

Veronica left the dining table and headed to his bedroom, which was on the same level. She entered the massive space expertly furnished in shades of pale blues and browns and headed to the closest nightstand.

She opened the first drawer. There was a long green box in it, yet no pen. Maybe it was in the box. She pulled out the box and opened it.

Veronica went cold inside. "Jude?" she called out in a shaky voice.

Something about her voice must have made Jude rush in. "What is it?"

Veronica turned and faced him, her whole body shaking like a leaf. "Where did you get this?"

"This pendant?" She nodded. "Remember the girl that saved my life? She gave it to me."

"At a hospital."

Jude stared at her in surprise. "How did you know?"

"And she gave you a lollipop?"

"How did… That's you?"

"Yes. You were leaning against a tree and kicking stones with your foot."

"But you have no mole on your arm."

"You checked?"

Jude nodded. "I wondered at one time."

"I had it removed a couple years ago."

Jude slumped in the armchair in the room and ran a hand over his hair. "Wow! I can't believe it. I've been searching for you all this time, yet you've been right here in front of me all along."

Veronica pulled out the pendant hidden under her dress. "Here's the other half of the pendant. I haven't worn it in a while, but I wore it today since it matched my dress." She removed it and then synced it with the pendant in the box. It was a match.

Just like they were together.

Who would have thought Jude was that boy

she'd liked at first sight, the one she'd wanted to wipe away the frown on his face?

Jude pulled her into his lap. "I'm so glad I finally found you," he whispered. "Thank you for giving me hope so many years ago. I love you, Vee."

Veronica hugged him right back. "I love you, Jude."

Then Jude kissed her to prove he meant every word.

The Christmas jinx had truly been a lie. Instead, Veronica had found the love of her life, and a family that was truly her own.

Including her very own Billionaire Dentist.

"How does it look?" Jude asked Veronica. They were standing in front of Veronica's clinic and a new sign had been put up.

"It looks awesome." The name "Fuller Dental" had been replaced by "Fuller-Brooks Dental." Veronica had wanted to pay homage to the many years Dr. Fuller had put in to build the practice, even though she now owned the clinic one hundred percent. Jude had offered to help her buy Dr. Fuller's share of the practice, but Veronica had opted to take a loan from him instead and pay it off over time. She'd wanted to earn it with her hard work.

Jude had also renovated the building faster

than Veronica had expected, and now, a month later, the place looked amazing. She'd been able to make all the upgrades she'd wanted since the clinic was now hers. Even though the clinic had never really closed, Veronica planned to reopen the clinic tomorrow with some fanfare. Sheila, as usual, had been on top of the planning. Veronica hadn't hired a new orthodontist just yet—Jude's orthodontist came over to Veronica's clinic on the days her patients had their appointments, and the arrangement had worked well so far.

"I want to make a proposal," Jude said.

"Again? You already proposed a month ago."

Jude chuckled. "Not that kind of proposal. What if we had a collaborative agreement where I send my pediatric patients who need specialized care to you, and you send your dental surgical cases to me? What do you think?"

What did she think? She'd always sent out their surgical cases to specialists, so it wasn't a loss for her. Instead she'd get a chance to see more patients in her specialty, which was something she'd always wanted. "That would be perfect!"

"Great. I'll have Tyler liaise with my lawyers

to draw up an agreement and then send it to your lawyers to review."

"Thank you."

"I have something else for you," Jude said, taking her hand and placing a large envelope on it.

"What is it?" Veronica asked looking from the envelope to Jude.

"Open it and see."

Veronica unfastened the string around the envelope's button and flipped the flap open. She pulled out a sheet of paper from it, read it, and gasped. "How—"

"Happy belated engagement present, darling," Jude said. "You're now the new owner of this building."

"But—"

He placed a finger on her lips. "No buts."

Tears pooled in her eyes. When the Christmas season had come around a few weeks ago, Veronica had never imagined a new love, a new family, a budding practice, and now a new building. God indeed had been gracious to her. "Thank you," she said and wrapped her arms around him.

Jude kissed the top of her head. "You're welcome, baby."

Veronica's heart was full. Her life had turned out way better than her beginning had suggested it would.

Thank you so much for reading! Want to know what happens next in Dexington where Phillip's and Sarah's son, Blake, found love (an enemies-to-lovers romance)?

Check out LOVING THE BILLIONAIRE HEIR DOC at https://dobidaniels.com.

Here's an excerpt:

Just then, Blake heard a shout. He turned his head to see a dark-haired, long-legged beauty hollering like a banshee and headed full speed in his direction. If he wasn't in a hurry, it would have been amusing. As she got closer, Blake could barely make out what she was saying. "Hey, you!" he heard her yell.

Blake looked behind him. There was no

one standing there. It seemed he was the target of this human tornado.

The young lady barreled closer with her hair whipped all over her face—he couldn't make out her features. Her stained medical coat failed to hide her lithe, gorgeous figure.

Blake felt a jolt in his system, and his heart raced. She was stunning, even though she seemed mad about something. He sucked in a quick breath. *What's going on?* he thought. It had been a long time since he'd felt this way.

"Here you go," a voice said beside him, bringing him back to reality. A young man in a valet uniform held out a ticket to him. Blake gave him a brief smile and accepted the ticket in exchange for his car keys.

He looked at his watch. One minute left. He wished there was more time; it would have been fascinating to find out what the bombshell wanted with him.

Casting a regretful glance at her, Blake turned and sprinted toward the hospital entrance and through its revolving doors...

Want to read more? You can grab LOVING THE

BILLIONAIRE HEIR DOC at
https://dobidaniels.com!

Or want to know what happens next in
Dexington?
Sign up now at https://dobidaniels.com.

If you've loved reading A Billionaire Dentist for
Christmas, Dobi would be grateful if you could
spend a few minutes to leave a review (as short
as you like) on the book's page on your favorite
retailer. Your review would help bring it to the
attention of other readers. Thank you very
much.

Check out all Dobi Daniels books at
https://dobidaniels.com

ACKNOWLEDGMENTS

Writing a book is harder and more rewarding than I could have ever imagined. And it would not have been possible without the support, love, and encouragement from my number one cheerleader, my dearest mom. My life would never have been this awesome and wonderful without you.

Of course, I have to thank my precious little DC for his smiles and antics. You brighten my day and give me the strength to keep pushing through.

Thank you to my sisters for encouraging me on this wonderful journey. And a special thanks to my baby brother (who is so not a baby anymore) for being super supportive and checking in on my progress. You guys are the best.

Thank you to my wonderful author friends. You know who you are. Your selflessness and willingness to share what you know has made my writing journey smoother and an exciting one. And a special thanks to my ARC readers whose support have made a difference.

Most of all, I want to thank God who gave me life, surrounded me with the most wonderful people, and loved me all the way. You make my life complete.

And finally, a special thanks to all my readers whose love of my stories spur me on to write more. Thank you!

As a former physician and business executive in another life—with a childhood filled with reading multi-genre novels—Dobi Daniels loves to write sweet thrilling romance stories with heart. She enjoys dreaming up everyday characters who rise above unfavorable circumstances to overcome incredible odds and find joy along the way.

When not writing, Dobi can be found binging K-dramas and ice cream with her little sidekick by her side.

A Billionaire Dentist for Christmas is the third book in the Dexington Christmas Billionaires Series. Sign up at dobidaniels.com to be notified when the next Dobi Daniels book comes out!

Thank you!

www.dobidaniels.com
hello@dobidaniels.com
facebook.com / dobidaniels
bookbub.com / profile / dobi-daniels
instagram.com / dobidaniels